MINE TO PROTECT

SAFE HARBOR SERIES

JEN TALTY

JUPITER PRESS

This book is a work of fiction. Names, characters, places, and incidents are products of the author's imagination or used fictitiously. Any resemblance to actual events or locales or persons living or dead is entirely coincidental.

Copyright © 2020 by Jen Talty All rights reserved.

No part of this work may be used, stored, reproduced or transmitted without written permission from the publisher except for brief quotations for review purposes as permitted by law. This book is licensed for your personal enjoyment only. This book may not be re-sold or given away to other people. If you would like to share this book with another person, please purchase an additional copy for each recipient. If you're reading this book and did not purchase it, or it was not purchased for your use only, please purchase your own copy.

Originally published by Lady Boss Press.

the NYS Troopers series." *Long and Short Reviews*

"*In Two Weeks* hooks the reader from page one. This is a fast paced story where the development of the romance grabs you emotionally and the suspense keeps you sitting on the edge of your chair. Great characters, great writing, and a believable plot that can be a warning to all of us." *Desiree Holt, USA Today Bestseller*

"*Dark Water* delivers an engaging portrait of wounded hearts as the memorable characters take you on a healing journey of love. A mysterious death brings danger and intrigue into the drama, while sultry passions brew into a believable plot that melts the reader's heart. Jen Talty pens an entertaining romance that grips the heart as the colorful and dangerous story unfolds into a chilling ending." *Night Owl Reviews*

"This is not the typical love story, nor is it the typical mystery. The characters are well rounded and interesting." *You Gotta Read Reviews*

"Murder in Paradise Bay is a fast-paced romantic thriller with plenty of twists and turns to keep you guessing until the end. You won't want to miss this one..." *USA Today bestselling author Janice Maynard*

MINE TO PROTECT

A SAFE HARBOR NOVEL

USA Today Bestseller
JEN TALTY

1

---

*S*helby Manzo gripped her cell as she sat in her brother's hotel room, which looked like a twister had touched down in the center and snaked through the space while doing as much damage as possible. Her heart hammered in the center of her chest. She blinked and did her best to take a deep breath, though her lungs didn't completely inflate with oxygen. She glanced around the room again. Some of her brother's things were on the bed, while a pair of pants and two shirts were bunched up on the floor.

That wasn't like Chris. To call him a neat freak would be a total understatement. He was the kind of person that, if she moved a lamp in his family room and he walked in, he'd notice in a heartbeat and fix it just as fast.

At least, sober Chris would.

Her heart rate kicked up, pushing against her rib cage. The acid in her gut was churning double-time. The worry over her brother consumed her both emotionally and physically. She rubbed her hands together in a lame attempt to keep them from shaking. She couldn't believe her brother would go missing in Lighthouse Cove, of all places. It was as if he'd decided to land in the one place where her past would collide with her present in a ball of wicked fire, twisting her insides and making it impossible to take a normal breath.

And of all the cops who might take the call, it would be someone related to Rhett Kirby.

Her mind flew back to Key West for a brief moment.

The sun.

The sand.

And Rhett.

He'd been so attentive, and yet he'd given her all the space and freedom she'd never had before. Those three short weeks had shown her what everyone else in the world had. She put those memories in a little box and cherished them.

Shelby squared her shoulders and forced herself back to the present.

Part of her was grateful for the Kirby family. For their familiarity. Rhett had spoken highly of his police brothers.

And mother.

The fact that they'd come to the hotel to go through it with her, told her there was some merit to her concern.

She shivered. If Chris was using, his disappearance wasn't necessarily criminal, and she knew that. However, something in the back of her mind told her that things didn't add up.

"You mentioned that you tried to file a missing persons report on"—Emmerson Kirby glanced at his notepad—"Chris. When was that?"

"Two days ago when I noticed his phone was turned off."

"Why?"

"Because I hadn't heard from him for two days before that," she said.

"Is that unusual?" Emmerson asked.

"Very," she said. "We talk almost every day, even if it's just one or two texts. But he didn't respond. Or answer my calls. So, I tried tracking him. That's when I noticed it was turned off."

"Do you always track your brother's phone?" Emmerson asked.

She'd only met one of Rhett's brothers during their short love affair—if one could call it that—and that had been Emmett, not Emmerson, though by the looks of it, they were nearly interchangeable in looks and personality, at least to a certain degree.

When she met Rhett, he had been following some guy for Emmett while in Key West. They'd turned it into a game, and Shelby had loved it. She'd enjoyed playing private eye with Rhett. She'd never experienced that kind of rush before in all her life. It made her heart pump like a lion waiting to pounce on its prey.

At the time, she hadn't known she'd been falling in love with Rhett. She'd thought she was simply getting lost in the moment. Not giving her soul to a man. However, when she packed her suitcase and tossed it into the back of her car, her heart broke into a million pieces. The entire ride back north was filled with guttural sobs and the kind of physical pain that she didn't think would ever go away. However, she had a brother to take care of and a life to get back to.

She breathed in slowly through her nose as Emmett rummaged through her brother's things in the bathroom with a pair of gloves, and Rhett's mother stood outside the hotel room. It felt as though they were treating the room like a crime scene. She wasn't sure if that was a good or a bad thing. But it made her feel as though her brother was the criminal. Not the victim.

At least they were taking it all seriously—unlike the police officer in Jacksonville.

"Yes," she said. "He could track me, as well." She didn't know why she felt the need to tell Emmerson that, but it somehow made it seem less weird. Many families used the find my device apps for various reasons, whether it be for safety, to spy, or to see why a friend was late. It was a helpful tool. She and Chris used to joke about how they should turn it off. But they hadn't. They'd both agreed that it gave them a sense of connectivity—especially after their father died.

Chris also admitted that it gave him comfort that at least one person always knew where he was…just in case.

"You filed that report with the Jacksonville County Sheriff's office, right?" Emmerson asked.

She nodded.

"And what did they do?"

She shrugged. "Not much of anything."

"What did you tell them?"

"I told them that Chris and I speak almost every day, even if it's just in text. When he goes off-grid, that's when I know he's using. But he hasn't done that in five years. They told me there wasn't much they could do."

"That was the last time he used drugs?" Emmerson asked. "That you know of."

"Yes." The irony in that statement had her head spinning. After she'd left Key West, she'd stared at her phone for months, waiting for Rhett's call. But it never came. She'd written in her journal about her time with him and what it meant to her, and how those memories filled her heart.

She wrote about how she wished she had the courage to call him but couldn't. Not because she thought a woman shouldn't call a man—that would be silly and stupid. But a part of Rhett seemed untouchable. Unreachable.

He'd closed off a piece of his heart to her—to the world—and that scared her because it was the piece that made a person whole.

She knew because she couldn't share that part of herself either.

She'd tried for three weeks and failed.

But those days in Key West…she could forget

her troubles. Forget about her father and brother and focus on nothing but losing herself in the fantasy she'd created with Rhett. It had been like being on a romantic adventure created by a romance writer. It had a beginning. It had a middle. And it had an ending.

Only it didn't have the happily ever after.

But she had the memories. She often looked back on those three weeks and knew that it was what love and life were supposed to be like— *could* be like if she were anyone else.

As a little girl, she'd dreamt of having a boyfriend that would come and sweep her off her feet and take her away from all her troubles.

But that could never happen for her, and not only because of her brother. So many things in life ended up getting in the way of true love. She kept telling herself that she'd chase that dream someday.

But when the right man came along, it'd happened at the worst possible time.

"Has the Jacksonville Police Department followed up?"

"I've checked in with them." Unfortunately, they didn't seem to be as detailed in their questioning, listening, or how they responded. One of the cops knew her brother from his using days.

That hadn't helped.

"We'd like to speak with the officer who took the report and see what they've been doing."

She let out a short laugh. "I'm sorry, but they aren't doing anything to investigate it. They even told me he was probably on a bender and would show up when he needed money. Unfortunately, my brother has a long history with our local law enforcement, and it's not positive. Though, as I said, he's been clean for five years." She felt like she needed to repeat that, and not just to herself.

"Regardless, we'll want to check with them." Emmerson gave her a reassuring nod and glanced around. "This room is in shambles. Does your brother normally live like this?"

"No. He's a neat freak—when he's sober."

Emmerson wrote something in his notepad.

A noise caught her attention, and she glanced over her shoulder. Her breath hitched. Her pulse raced out of control like a fish flopping on a dock, desperate to get back in the water. A rush of heat coated her skin as if she'd been hit with a hose filled with fire.

Rhett Kirby stood in the hotel room's doorway. He wore a pair of dark jeans, boots, and a black T-shirt. He pushed his sunglasses onto the top of his head, taking some of his long, thick, wavy hair with them. He smiled. It seemed as if he focused only on her, and that made the room spin.

"Hey, Shelby," he said in a low voice. It rumbled from his throat and flowed through the air, landing on her muscles and rippling across them like a soft breeze.

She opened her mouth as if to taste his essence, then swallowed. "Hi," she managed in a whisper. Visions of learning how to surf and laughing so hard her belly hurt appeared in her head. Rhett had absorbed all the pain that'd filled her mind and soul five years ago. He'd given her an outlet for her fears. He'd shown her a world without worry and preoccupation. Somewhere that was all hers and didn't include taking care of everyone else.

But it had all been an illusion.

She might have fallen in love, but both she and Rhett were not made for lasting relationships. She understood that about herself, and she suspected that maybe he did, too. Perhaps that was why he didn't call. Or, more likely, he just didn't care for her the same way. And that was okay.

"You told my brother Emmett that during your last conversation with Chris, he sounded off. What did you mean by that?" Emmerson asked, jerking her from the safe haven of her past with Rhett, a place she only dared to go late at night when she was by herself—or when she chose to journal. Rhett was the one thing she didn't share with anyone. He'd become that happy place that every therapist asked her to create.

She ripped her gaze away from Rhett. Rhett had visited her in her dreams for months after she left Key West, but as much as she'd wanted to call him, dealing with the day-to-day life of her family had been all she could handle. Once Chris had gotten on the right track, she'd told herself that she would reach out but then found herself coming up with one excuse after another. Months passed. Then a year. Then two. Then three. Then her father's cancer had returned. Her family was all she had, and she couldn't add a man to the mix.

Her therapist had told her it had nothing to do with her taking care of her family and doing what was right for them, and more to do with sticking with a role she'd been given and not stepping out of that comfort zone—which wasn't a healthy choice. Being the caregiver for her family while not taking care of her own needs wasn't her responsibility for life.

But someone had to do it.

"He was agitated. Paranoid." *Just like when he used to use.* She hated even having that thought. Chris had been doing so well. He had a job, a girlfriend, and money in the bank. Even when he had setbacks in life, he worked them out.

"I need you to be more specific," Emmerson said.

For most of her life, Shelby had been a private person. She didn't like sharing details of her personal life with anyone, including her best friends —especially things about her brother. That was his business. It wasn't that she was ashamed. Far from it. But it made other people uncomfortable, and she didn't feel like dealing with idiots. Besides, that was what you paid a therapist for.

"Our father died a year ago. My brother really struggled for the first few months, but he pulled his shit together. Until about six weeks ago when he started to behave oddly. He would get pissed at me for no reason, or snap at me if I questioned him. I caught him sneaking around my house a couple of times. It was like dealing with him before the real shit hit the fan five years ago."

"Did something else change in his life?" Rhett asked as he leaned against the doorjamb.

"He took a job at his girlfriend's family's limo

company. But it was a good job. Only…that's when I noticed the changes." She caught Rhett's gaze.

His intense eyes had always captivated her in ways that touched her core. It was as if he could see right into her soul without even trying. It scared her because he had a way of knowing her thoughts and feelings.

"How did he change?" Rhett asked softly.

"He got secretive and started pulling away. He used the excuse that he'd been clean and sober for five years and was sick and tired of his older sister not trusting him, which was total bullshit. We were past all that." She held in a sob. Fear gripped her veins, squeezing the blood right out. She shook from the inside.

"When was the last time you actually saw him?" Rhett asked in a kind and soft tone.

Tears burned a path down her cheeks at the reminder of the ugly fight she'd gotten into with Chris. "Six days ago," she said. This was no time to keep secrets. She needed help. Her brother needed help. "We fought because I found him and his girl-friend in my house."

"Do they need your permission?" Emmerson asked. "Because my brothers come and go pretty much as they please."

"He's got a key, but he's always been respectful. This time, I caught him in my office, going through my things. The last time he did that was a little over five years ago when he tried to steal my mom's wedding rings and some other jewelry so he could pawn them to buy drugs."

"Did he take anything from your house that day?" Emmerson asked.

"Not that I could find," she said. "And, trust me, I checked everything."

"What kind of things do you keep in your office?" Rhett asked. "Is there a safe? Checkbooks? Keys to safety deposit boxes that have valuable things in them?"

"Mostly paperwork." Her cheeks heated as she thought about all the things she'd written about Rhett. She'd filled at least half a dozen journals with thoughts about him. It bordered on obsessive. "The safe is in my bedroom closet."

Emmett stepped into the main area of the hotel room. "There's nothing unusual in the bathroom. It's just really messy, which could be because they are on vacation and don't want to clean up after themselves. Or something else. Especially since half the contents of the cosmetic kit were on the floor," he said.

"What do you mean something else?" she asked.

"I don't like the way the room looks. It's almost as if someone went through their things, tossing them about as if they were looking for something," Emmett said. "We'll talk with the manager at the hotel, but there's something else of note. Your brother and his girlfriend left everything behind, including their electronics. We found both cell phones, a tablet, and a laptop." Emmett pointed to the ladies' clothing on the bed. "Tell me about the girlfriend."

Shelby wanted to ask more about who might have come in and searched her brother's room, but her brain could barely function enough to answer their questions. "She's nice. I like her. She's kind of quiet, and I wish I knew her better. Her uncle's the one who gave my brother the job."

"Did you file a report on her, as well?" Rhett asked.

Shelby blew out a puff of air. "I did."

"What about her family? Did they?" Emmerson asked.

"Both her parents died when she was little. Her uncle raised her. I left a message with the limo company but never heard back from him. Which is weird. But the person who answered the phone told me they thought my brother and Jackie were on vacation." She rubbed her temple. "Don't you find it strange that they would leave their phones and stuff behind?" Her heart beat so fast she thought it might jump right out of her chest, through her throat, and out her mouth like a flying fish. "Why would they do that?"

"That's a good question," Emmerson said. "You mentioned that the hotel called you to come collect your brother's things because he left them behind, but when you got here, they said that wasn't true."

"That's right." She'd been furious at the clerk and the manager and finally decided to just go knock on the door. "I spent last night here. When my brother and Jackie didn't return, the manager let me in, and I called you."

"Why didn't you call me last night?" Rhett asked with a tight jaw.

"It was late. Besides, I wanted to stay here so I could see if he came back. Which, obviously, he didn't."

"Does your brother always carry this much money with him?" Emmett held up some cash.

"No. Not usually," she said.

"And what about his car? Have you seen it at all since you got here?" Emmerson shifted his stance, moving closer toward the bathroom and sticking his head inside.

"No. And I drove around town looking for it, too," she said.

"We'll need the make, model, and license plate if you have it," Emmerson said.

"Not a problem." She choked on a sob. Having Rhett and his family here made all of this too real. Yet she kept wondering when she would wake up from this nightmare.

Emmett narrowed his eyes as he took a hundred-dollar bill and held it up to the light. "I think we have a different problem here."

"What's that?" Rhett asked.

"This is counterfeit." Carefully, Emmett set it on the table. "It's time to take this conversation outside. We'd better get Mom in here."

"Counterfeit?" What the hell was her brother doing with fake money? That didn't make any sense.

"Come on." Rhett held out his hand. "There's a picnic table in the courtyard. My mom's got the place blocked off. We can go sit there, and these guys can do their job here."

"That's a good idea," Emmett said. "This could

change things from a simple missing person to something else entirely."

"Like what?" She stood, shifting her gaze between the two men in uniform to Rhett. "What's going on? I don't understand. My brother's missing, and I want to find him."

"That money changes things." He pointed at the hundred. "It gives us something else to look at. But we need some space to do our jobs," Emmerson said.

It made her brother look like a bad person.

"Let's go." Rhett pressed his hand to the small of her back and guided her through the door, right past a woman with long, blond hair wearing a uniform, barking orders to everyone in sight. The woman paused for a moment and smiled at Rhett.

"Hey, Ma," Rhett said. "We'll be right over there." He pointed to a grassy area that had a couple of tables.

"That's fine. I'll need to talk to her in a bit," his mother said.

What the hell had her brother done?

She took in a deep, cleansing breath and glanced around.

The hotel itself was on the outskirts of Lighthouse

Cove, about eight miles from the ocean, closer to the river but not on the water. It was kind of a dingy hotel but clean. And affordable. But it wasn't a dump. Chris had been trying to save some money since he'd been broke for most of his life. Up until he'd been about thirty years old, he'd been paying off old debt. Now, at thirty-three, he was finally in a position where he wasn't always living paycheck to paycheck.

But it was close.

"It's been a long time," Rhett said.

"Five years." She tucked her hair behind her ears and sat with the sun behind her back since she had no idea where her sunglasses were. Besides, as crazy as it sounded, it gave her a chance to check Rhett out. Seemed odd under the circumstances, but she needed something to settle her nerves, and Rhett had always been good at that. She felt a pang of guilt for using him in that way. However, her heart hurt, and she needed a little relief. "Your hair is longer."

He ran his hand through his dark, shoulder-length hair. "It drives my mom nuts. Of course, the fact that I'm not a cop is still a sore subject with her, but it's worse for my little brother Miles."

"Ah. The mechanic." She smiled.

"He also does some work for me," Rhett said.

"Isn't there a lawyer and a firefighter, too?"

"I'm impressed. You remember."

Her cheeks heated. She remembered everything about those three weeks in Key West. It wasn't just because Rhett had given her a way to deal with her worry over her brother; he had filled her heart with pure joy and passion. It was something she'd never experienced before, and because of her family life with her brother and father, she hadn't had the opportunity for it to ever happen again.

Her therapist had told her that before she knew Rhett, she'd chosen men who left her feeling unfulfilled. She picked guys that, while kind and good men, could never feed her emotions the way a relationship should.

And after she'd experienced Rhett, her standards became impossible. No man could ever live up to what she wanted. Therefore, all her experiences ended before they even began.

"But you never told me you had a brother," he said.

There were many things she hadn't told Rhett about her life during those three glorious weeks. She hadn't wanted to ruin what they had with deep, intense conversations about things that would bring tears to her eyes and dampen all the excitement over the things she'd never been exposed to before. All she wanted was time to escape, and Rhett had given that to her in spades.

He'd shown her around Key West, took her fishing, sailing, snorkeling. Anything that could be done, they did it.

And the sex had been mind-blowing. She'd had no idea that she could be that sensual or wild between the sheets.

However, the truth of the matter was that she'd left all of that—and her heart—in Key West.

It had been the only time in her life when she'd given herself permission to be selfish. Love wasn't something that came easily to her, but she'd fallen in love with Rhett as if it were the most natural thing in the world to do. To this day, Rhett came and visited each time she closed her eyes at night. She remembered every tender touch. Every sweet kiss. Every kind word.

"I didn't tell you a lot of things," she admitted. "And you never called, even though you said you would."

He tapped the center of his chest. "I guess I deserve that."

"I didn't mean for it to be a competition. What we had was a long time ago, and it was a fling. We were never meant to last." The words might have rolled off her tongue with ease, but a sudden burn churned in the center of her chest. Not a day had gone by since her trip to Key West that she hadn't thought about Rhett. She'd even gone so far as to search for him on the internet. A bit out of curiosity, and in part because she wanted to know if he had a good life. That was important to her—for all the people she cared about.

It was something her therapist told her she needed to do for herself.

She'd found a few articles. Images. And some stories about his family. She'd savored every single one, and when her father had taken his last breath, the memory of Rhett had eased her soul and brought her comfort in her darkest hour.

Unfortunately, that never took away her heartache for the man she knew she loved but could never have. Of course, never in a million years did she think she would see him again. And, yet, here she was, sitting next to him on a bench in Lighthouse Cove, Florida. It stirred all the same feelings deep in the pit of her stomach. Her fingers itched to touch him. Her lips were desperate to kiss him.

But that would never happen again.

That ship had sailed a long time ago.

Rhett glanced toward the hotel room. "Do you have any idea how your brother got a hold of counterfeit money?"

"I wish I did."

"What about his girlfriend? What's her name?"

"Jackie Staub." Shelby tried not to trip over the last name. There were a couple of rumors around town that Jackie's uncle had ties to some local mob family—the Mortellis. Shelby had checked it out on the internet, but not much had come up. Only a couple of articles. At first, she'd been concerned and brought it to her brother's attention. He'd blown it off as people making trouble where there was none and explained that her uncle and parents had grown up in New Jersey in a tough neighborhood. After her parents had been murdered, and the case went unsolved, her uncle had been concerned that it might have been mob-related, so he moved Jackie to Florida.

But the rumors followed them. And then there was the fact that her uncle had struggled financially at first and might have taken a loan from the Mortelli family. But that was all water under the bridge. He'd made a business for himself and turned it all around.

So, she googled *that* and didn't find much of

anything. She didn't know Jackie well, but what she did know, she liked. And her brother was happy and healthy and doing great.

Until six weeks ago, when everything changed.

"Does she have any of the same issues your brother has?"

"Not that I know of," Shelby said. "They have been dating for about six months, and she seems like a really sweet girl. Thanks to her, Chris was able to get a job in her uncle's company as a manager. And Chris felt it was a career opportunity —or at least that's what he told me. But the second he took the position, everything got weird."

"What's the name of that company?"

"Florida Five Star," she said. "Shouldn't I be giving all this to your brothers?"

"I'll make sure they have it. Anything else they may need in a formal statement, they will ask you for it." Rhett shifted closer. "We'll work together, but I can do some things they can't."

"I would think it would be the other way around."

Rhett chuckled. "Their badge restricts them in some ways. For things to hold up in a court of law, it must be by the book. I get to skirt those laws. But I have to be careful. It's a fine line."

"Don't you have to first believe my brother is missing? And then don't I have to hire you?" She kept coming back to the original phone call the hotel had supposedly made—which it turned out they hadn't.

That bothered her. Because if a clerk hadn't called her to come and get her brother's things, who had? And why?

He took her hand. "First, based on what we saw back there, the way the place was torn apart, and the fact that all his stuff was left behind, we all believe something isn't right. And not just because of the counterfeit money. He could have picked that up anywhere."

"I don't understand why the hotel would call me and then lie about it."

"My brothers will investigate that. As will I. Which brings me to my second point. You're not paying me to look for your brother. I want to help you. Besides, my brothers will be asking for my assistance anyway. It's how my family rolls. Like when I was in Key West doing that favor for Emmett."

"Thank you. But I insist on paying. That's how *I* roll."

"We'll talk about that later." He leaned in and

brushed his lips across her cheek. "I'm very sorry for the circumstances, but it is good to see you again."

She had to admit, it was more than good to see him. She held his gaze for a long moment, unsure what to say.

Or what to do.

His tongue made a broad stroke across his plump lips.

"We're going to find him and his girlfriend." Rhett squeezed her biceps. "I'm not going to rest until we do."

"Hey, Rhett." A woman's voice rang out from near the side of the hotel. "I need to speak with you."

"I'd better go see what my mom wants," he said. "You hang tight right here. I'll be back shortly."

She grabbed his hand. "I'm scared for him."

"I wish I could tell you not to be." He stood and strolled toward his mother.

She turned and stared off at the sun in the bright blue Florida sky, trying to project her thoughts as strongly as she could to her brother. "Please, Chris. Let me know you're okay."

Rhett's mother had two modes.

Cop.

And chief of police.

There was no fucking in-between.

Growing up, he'd been held to a higher standard than every other kid in Lighthouse Cove and, frankly, it'd sucked. He and the second youngest brother, Miles, rebelled against that authority the most. Rhett had been the first one to get a tattoo. He'd been the first one to grow his hair longer than police regulation and absolutely refuse to get it cut.

He'd used his pool-cleaning money to buy a motorcycle when he was sixteen, and his mother had grounded him for life.

Rhett never did anything that would get him into too much trouble, though. Sure, he'd stolen some beer from his parents' fridge, and he'd smoked a little weed in high school, but he'd learned at a very young age how to walk that fine line between being a rebel and actually doing something his mother would have to arrest him for. However, he moved out once he hit eighteen. He'd needed breathing space. He was the son that needed to make all his own decisions. While his eldest brother followed in their father's footsteps, and three of his brothers were cops, Rhett had needed to do something different.

But not *that* different.

Not like Miles, who everyone thought their mother would totally disown at one point when he continued tinkering with cars and not guns. However, that didn't stop their mom from giving Rhett shit and fighting him every chance she got when he opted to become a private investigator. But that skill came in handy, and she'd hired him three weeks after he got his license.

"Hotel management is giving us their phone records. They are adamant that they didn't call the sister."

"Someone did," Rhett said. "Did you find anything other than one counterfeit bill?"

"A couple of things," his mom said. "There's a business card in his wallet indicating that he works —or worked—at Florida Five Star."

"I know. Shelby told me that."

His mom tilted her head and arched her brow. That look meant one of two things. Either she was annoyed by his response, or she expected him to know what she was eluding to and he didn't.

"I take it that's important?" Rhett shifted his

stance so he could see Shelby. She hadn't moved from her spot on the bench. The sun hit her long hair, creating a shiny glow. She looked exactly as he remembered and was as beautiful as the most exquisite piece of art without being pretentious. During their time together, she'd often been slightly timid about their adventures, but she was always willing to try something new.

He'd loved that about her.

It saddened him that her soul still had that deep, gut-wrenching anguish he'd seen in her five years ago. Back then, he'd probably had it, too. He'd gone to Key West because Emmett had needed him to follow someone for a case. But the reality was, he was still dealing with a broken heart, and he'd just found out that his ex-girlfriend had gotten married. He'd been holding out hope that Krista would one day come back to him—for good—but when she got hitched, he'd had to face the fact that that part of his life was over.

Only he hadn't expected to fall in love with Shelby, and in such a short time, and that had been utterly terrifying. When he realized what had happened, he did whatever it took to protect his heart—and that meant moving on and forgetting all about her.

Only, he never did. No matter how hard he tried, she haunted his dreams and seeped into his daily thoughts.

"Joe Staub owns it," his mother said.

"Isn't that the girlfriend's uncle? Is that name supposed to mean something more?"

"He's been tagged recently as having a possible connection to Hector Mortelli. There was one twenty-seven years ago, but he's been clean. Until recently."

Now *that* was a name Rhett knew, and it wasn't someone anyone should be spending time with unless they wanted to end up in prison. Or dead. "How recently?"

"I'm not exactly sure. It's chatter on the streets. I'm trying to work through it, but you know I've been building a case to bring those assholes down."

"Fuck," Rhett mumbled. "So, our missing brother is dating the niece of a potential mob connection." This would not go over well with Shelby.

Then again, he realized the woman he'd thought he knew in Key West, wasn't the woman he was dealing with now.

"That's the way it's looking." His mother stared at him with that intense gaze she got when she wanted the total truth and nothing but. "However, we don't know the connection."

And she had a way of making him tell it, even when he wanted to bottle it up and save it for later.

Or for never.

"How well do you know this girl?"

He swallowed. He and his mom had developed an understanding over the years. He often kept certain facts from her to protect the integrity of an investigation. However, he had no idea what the hell was going on with Chris, or if this was even criminal at this point. But lying to his mom right now didn't seem like a good idea. He also didn't have a good handle on Shelby or her family.

"I met her five years ago in Key West. We spent a few weeks together. That's about it."

His mother lowered her chin. "She's *that* girl?"

"What does that mean?" He really didn't need to ask that question because he knew, and he would have to have a conversation with one—or all of—his brothers. Sometimes, his family was just way too fucking close, which was odd because they were insanely dysfunctional.

"The one who had your head all turned around as bad as Krista. The one that helped you get over her but then—and the details are fuzzy because no one could tell me—you or her decided it wasn't worth pursuing." His mom took two steps to the right as if to block his view of the woman that occupied his brain. "And before you go getting pissed off at your brothers and start grilling them to find out which one told me, it took them a long time before they fessed up. And I had to bribe them— each and every one of them. And no one could give me the whole story."

That didn't necessarily make him feel any better, with one slight exception: both his parents chose to stay out of his business.

That was progress.

"What I don't understand is why you continue having meaningless one-night stands when we both know you're capable of a whole lot more," his mother said, glancing over her shoulder.

"I wouldn't call my relationships meaningless. And I think the girls I date would take offense."

"Oh, please. You do that thing called friends with benefits. There is no emotional commitment. Meanwhile, that girl over there on the bench has your heart in a tight squeeze."

"No, she doesn't," he lied. "When I met her, I was upset over Krista getting married." That had hurt. A lot. He'd poured his heart and soul into his relationship with Krista. He'd even been willing to give up his private investigating business since she'd thought he needed something a little more secure. Not to mention, she'd wanted to move back to Savannah where her family lived.

He liked Georgia.

Or so he'd tried to tell himself.

And of all the places in that state, Savannah wasn't the worst. So, he'd agreed. Only Krista had decided that Rhett wasn't the man for her and ended the relationship. Three months later, she moved in with someone else.

"For the record, I like Shelby. She's a nice girl. But I'm not a forever kind of man."

"I'm sure she's great, but I know you're full of shit with that kind of talk," his mother said with a slight all-knowing scrunch of her nose. "What I want to know right now is did she ever lie to you? That you know of."

"Not sure I'd call it a lie, but I didn't know she had a brother. We were kind of busy doing things that didn't include chatting."

"Too much information, son." His mom waved her hand. "What was she doing in Key West?"

"I didn't know this then, but apparently her brother was in rehab up in Miami. She dropped him off, drove south, and was waiting for his release."

"What did she tell you then was her reason for being there?"

"An extended vacation," he admitted.

"For three weeks?" His mom cocked her head and gave him a questioning glare as if he should have wondered why a woman would have that much time off work—and why she'd choose to spend it all in one place.

In hindsight, he *should* have questioned it. "At the time, I was preoccupied. I was working through my personal shit with Krista and keeping tabs on someone for Emmett. I know I should have thought about that detail, but it's not something we need to be concerned about."

"That we know of," his mother said. "What did you tell her?"

"She knew I was there working on something for Emmett."

His mother arched a brow. "You brought her into your work?"

"It wasn't a dangerous case," Rhett said.

His mom gave him a disapproving head shake. "I have no reason to ask her to stay in the imme-diate area. The only criminal connection I have is that counterfeit bill. But that doesn't have anything to do with her, and while it's clear the place was ransacked, there is no proof. They could have been messy vacationers. But something smells godawful about this."

"I agree. Which is why I'm going to ask her to stick around, and why I plan on taking the case."

"Good, because I honestly don't have the resources to make this a priority. Not when I've got boatloads of drugs coming in from the Keys again in the form of old-fashioned square groupers."

Rhett chuckled. "Mom. No one uses that term for marijuana being tossed from an airplane and having it wash up on shore anymore."

"I just did," his mom said with a bright smile. "Now, go make sure she stays in town."

"I've got this. And I'll keep you in the loop."

His mother squeezed his shoulder. "Just don't cross a bunch of lines. And for God's sake, since you've already given her your heart, make sure she's not a criminal."

2

The older Rhett got, the more his restless soul began to settle, even though he tried to fight it. Purchasing a house on the river was one step to becoming the adult his age indicated. When he signed on the dotted line two months ago, he'd thought his blood pressure would go through the roof. He'd been having heartburn for weeks, but moving in had been a kind of high he'd never had the pleasure of experiencing before. It wasn't the typical adrenaline rush that came on hard and left just as fast.

This was more of a slow-burn buildup that stuck with him for hours. Days, even.

One morning while making a cup of coffee, it'd hit him that he'd come home.

And when he parked his boat at the dock and had his brothers over to his tiki bar for a night of poker, it felt as though it was exactly where his life was supposed to land. He belonged in this spot. Nowhere else—even though he felt a twinge in his heart that something was missing.

But it was still weird to be a homeowner. Even stranger that he'd started driving his Jeep more than his motorcycle. The idea that he wasn't strapped to his bike had hit home a couple of times.

His daredevil ways weren't so much a death wish mentality as they were a way to avoid the realities of life. What'd started out as pushing the envelope as a kid had become a way to cope with the pain of a broken heart. After Key West, he'd realized that his eldest brother, Seth, had been right when he'd said that Rhett was letting life pass him by. His adventures, while amazing and accomplishments he should be proud of in his life, no longer gave him the same joy. They no longer soothed his aching heart.

However, he didn't know what settling down looked like for him because no one he'd dated made him feel the way Shelby had.

If he were being completely honest with himself, not even Krista had that effect on him. Of course, he'd loved Krista. That went without saying. But something about Shelby reached deep into his being and touched him in ways no one else ever did or could. He'd tried to forget her, but it'd never happened.

And the truth was, he never wanted to. Even if he spent the rest of his life alone, he was glad that he had the memories of Shelby.

"I don't think your mom likes me." Shelby took her food basket filled with a lobster roll and waffle fries and followed him to a picnic bench on the river. The Hungry Turtle had to be his favorite spot in all of Lighthouse Cove. As a kid, his big brother, Seth, would often take him fishing right off the fixed bridge. And on the days they didn't get even a single bite, Seth would treat him to his all-time favorite: clam strips and curly fries. It was only fitting that he would buy a house in a neighborhood not too far from this spot.

"It's not that at all." Rhett dug into his food. He hadn't had anything to eat in hours. "She's got a lot on her plate right now. Besides, missing persons cases are tough. If they don't have a good lead in twenty-four hours, the trail can become cold real quick, making her job even harder."

"And then no one is looking."

"I hate to say it, but that's a fact." He had a lot to discuss with Shelby, but he didn't want to get into the plethora of questions his mom and brothers had given him, not to mention his. Right now, he felt like dealing with the past. While he didn't feel as though she owed him anything since he had his answers for why she left, it seemed he owed *her* an explanation for why he'd ghosted her for five years. "All things considered, you look good."

"So do you." She smiled.

"You could have called me when you first thought your brother went missing," he said. "And you should have called me last night. I would have answered, and I certainly wouldn't have turned you away."

Her blue eyes picked up a ray of sunshine and lit up like the sky on the brightest day of summer.

He held her gaze, allowing himself this moment. His chest tightened, and it became difficult to fill his lungs with the salty air. He remembered lying in bed and staring into those orbs for what seemed like hours. When he first met her, twinges of guilt had haunted his thoughts. He'd bought her a drink at a tiki bar in part because she was the prettiest girl in the place, but also because she had a deep sadness about her, and he wanted to do his best to cheer her up.

He told himself it was because he understood the kind of emptiness that'd stared back at him from across the room, and misery loved company. In the first few hours of their initial meeting, he had only pure intentions. However, that'd quickly turned to lust, and it was mutual. Even though she'd never admitted it, he knew without a doubt that she'd been using him to drown her sorrows. He'd had no idea what her problems were at the time, and for the first week, he'd tried to convince himself that he didn't care.

However, the more time he spent with her, the more she mattered, and that meant he needed to push her away. He couldn't afford to swap one obsession for a new one.

Because that's what Krista had become. He hadn't been in love with Krista anymore. He'd become attached to the *idea* of her and refused to let her go. He'd used his unique skills to find out things about Krista, and the more he did that, the more he hated himself.

It bordered on stalking. He'd been ashamed of his behavior and needed to separate himself from it all. He didn't talk about it much, but he held onto what he'd thought was his love for Krista like a badge of honor, and all that did was make him a bitter old man before he turned thirty-eight. Now that he was forty-three, he refused to be that person, and even though Shelby had always been in the back of his mind, he chose to live and not dwell on someone he couldn't have.

Or at least not live the last five years like he was dying.

"To be honest, I thought about looking you up for advice regardless." She nibbled at her food.

"Why didn't you?"

"Because you never called." Her voice was neither combative nor sad, at least regarding him and his lack of communication. He shouldn't take it personally. She had a lot on her mind.

"I felt kind of foolish for thinking you would," she said with a layer of emotion.

He swallowed. He could use the excuse that he'd deleted her contact information all he wanted, but the truth of the matter was, he'd been too much of a chickenshit to use his great detective skills to find her. Because if he had, that meant he hadn't learned anything from the insanity of chasing Krista.

He wasn't a stalker. Never had been. He'd loved

a woman deeply, and she'd ripped his heart to shreds. And then dangled her love like a carrot in front of him, constantly teasing him, bringing him back, telling him that she'd made a mistake and wanted to make things right between them.

For two years after the initial breakup, before she got engaged but after she'd moved in with her new man, Krista would call him, crying about her boyfriend and how stifling the relationship had become. How controlling he was and how he bordered on abusive. She would tell Rhett that she was scared and didn't think she could leave. He'd beg her to get in her car and, a couple of times, she *did* drive back to Lighthouse Cove.

Both times she'd told Rhett that she'd broken up with her boyfriend, and Rhett had believed her, welcoming her back into his bed.

Big mistake. Because she went back to the guy weeks later, and Rhett worried for her safety all over again. However, it was all bullshit. She'd simply gotten cold feet.

"I was going through some stuff at the time." He mentally slapped himself upside the head as if he were a small child and his mother had caught him with his hand in the cookie jar. What had been going on in his life was no excuse for blowing someone off. He could have told her the truth. He could have been a man and been honest about his emotions.

"So was I." Her lips pursed.

He opened his mouth to remind her that she had his phone number and could have called him, too, but playing that game was childish and immature.

"I'm not hurt or angry. And if I'm being totally honest with you, when I went back to Jacksonville, I was hyper-focused on my brother. So, you not calling wasn't the end of the world."

Ouch. That hurt.

"But at the time, it would have been nice, considering we shared an intense three weeks."

It was impossible to keep from smiling as his mind tumbled back to five years ago and that bungalow in Key West.

"Confession time," he said. No way could he tell her that he'd fallen head over heels for her and that not a day passed where he didn't think about her and wonder what she was doing or if she had a boyfriend. If she was married. He quickly stole a glance at her ring finger.

No ring.

His heart pulsed a few extra beats.

He cleared his throat. This was not the time or place. Right now, he could give her some insight into his life when they met, and then he'd help her find her brother. Anything else would have to wait. "I wasn't totally upfront with you about why I was in Key West."

"You weren't there working a case?"

"I was, but I was also trying to get over a woman. Someone I'd been in love with, and I needed a distraction."

"Oh, really?" She lifted her paper cup and slurped from her straw. "So, you were using me."

He groaned. "That didn't come out right."

She laughed. "I think it's safe to say that we used each other. I dropped my brother off at a rehab facility and drove south with no real destination in mind. You provided me with a way to keep my mind off what he was going through. But, like I said, it would have been nice to hear from you."

"Communication works two ways, and you had my number, as well." He cringed. If he'd learned anything from any of his brothers and their relationships, it should have been that pushing a woman's buttons was the fastest way to get a palm across the cheek. "You could have reached out."

Apparently, he couldn't keep his mouth shut, though.

"I suppose I could have," she agreed. "Tell me about this chick you were getting over. Did it work, or are you back together?"

"The weekend I met you was the weekend she got married. We'd been on and off for so long that I kept thinking she would dump her fiancé. That never happened, and I was licking my wounds because I knew it was finally over."

"I'm sorry she broke your heart, but that doesn't answer why you never called me," Shelby said.

"I'm getting there."

She laughed. "You're taking the long way."

He generally didn't beat around the bush. He was known for getting to the point unless he was actively avoiding something. He didn't want to think about what he was circumventing at the moment because while his feelings for Shelby weren't as raw as they had been with Krista—in part because he'd kept them to himself—Shelby had no idea how he felt.

Krista did.

And Krista had sworn she felt the same way. Yet she'd married someone else.

Although that wasn't the point. He needed to

find a way to explain and apologize but not put everything out there.

"I want you to know it had nothing to do with you. I was in a bad personal space and had a lot of soul searching to do. It's taken me a long time to figure out who I am without Krista, and as much as I wanted to call you, I needed to learn to be alone."

"That's the girl you were getting over?"

He nodded. "It was an unhealthy relationship, and I had a destructive attachment to her. I couldn't be with anyone until I was good with being in my own skin."

"And how's that working out for you?"

He chuckled. "Pretty damn good." If she only knew how hard it was to sit across from her and not lean over, take her chin between his thumb and forefinger, and kiss the hell out of those pouty lips. Or how often he'd been with someone else and Shelby's face would pop into his mind.

It had been unfair to every woman he'd ever dated, which was why he preferred to immerse himself in work and have meaningless encounters with women who only wanted one thing from him.

He didn't mind being used. Hell, he preferred it that way.

He'd also decided that, at forty-three, he wasn't

marriage material—much to his mother's dismay. She wanted all her boys to get married and give her lots of grandchildren. So far, she had three from Seth, and two with one on the way from Nathan. Emmett and his fiancée planned to adopt. And Jamison and his wife had two kids and also wanted to adopt a child.

The fucking pressure on him, Emmerson, and Miles to reproduce in some fashion was often unbearable.

It was even worse when his dad got in on it.

As if they didn't have enough offspring who'd already reproduced.

"What about you? Anyone special in your life?" Acid filled the back of his throat. If she had someone, he wanted to know now. He *needed* to know. It would help him keep all the visions of holding her late at night in his new king-size bed that overlooked the open water at the end of the point at bay.

"Not currently."

Shit. That wasn't going to help.

However. He was a different man than he had been five years ago. He'd done the right thing by letting her go, and he could be professional now. But his mother wanted him to keep a close eye on her, which meant either he talked her into staying in his guest room...

Or Melinda, Emmett's ex-girlfriend, could put her up at the Landon Lighthouse Bed and Breakfast. But that meant sleeping in his Jeep. Again.

He really didn't want to do that.

But he would if he had to for the integrity of the case.

He glanced at his watch. It was pushing seven in the evening. It wasn't that long of a drive back up to Jacksonville, and she could easily do it, but that wasn't an option. He pushed his food to the side and reached across the table, resting his hand gently over hers. "I don't think it's a good idea for you to go home. Not just because it's late, but my brothers or mom might need to talk with you during the next day or two. And you might be able to aid me in my investigation. Remember, I can do things they can't."

"I was going to find a hotel."

"A family friend of mine has a bed and breakfast not far from here. I know she has a room, but I also live right around the corner. Why don't you stay with me?"

She narrowed her eyes, holding his gaze with a piercing stare as if the ocean had suddenly erupted in a storm. Her lips parted as if she were about to say something, so he waited for what seemed like ten minutes, only the birds making any noise.

He cleared his throat.

"I have a couple of nice guest rooms. A pool with a spa. I'm also right on the river. It would be easier for when I need you to answer questions."

"If I were to stay with you, I don't want you to think it would be a repeat of five years ago. I don't want that from you."

"I'm not suggesting that at all. I only want to help find your brother and his girlfriend."

Shelby's lashes fluttered over her big blue eyes. She nodded. "Okay. I'll stay with you. I appreciate the hospitality."

"My mom will feel much better about you staying with me than at the B&B."

"Why?" she asked.

Shit. He shouldn't have said that, and now he had to come up with something better than the fact that her brother might be sleeping with a member of a mob family. "My mom doesn't want anyone to feel uncomfortable, and if she or my brothers were coming and going from the bed and breakfast, that might make the guests uneasy."

"Oh. I see. That makes sense."

He stood, grabbing the empty trays of food. "Come on. You can follow me back to my place. While you get settled, I have a couple of errands to run. In the morning, we can go over everything you know about your brother's girlfriend and anything else you think may be important."

She jumped to her feet, raced around the table, and grabbed his arm. "Thank you for not thinking I'm crazy."

The oxygen in his lungs flew out like a jet screaming down a runway. It would take all his energy to keep his damn fucking hands to himself. Even wrapping his arms around her in comfort would be too dangerous.

Maybe he could explore a date after he found her brother.

But not until then.

This time, he'd do things right.

3

Shelby took her glass of wine and made herself comfortable in one of the chairs by the pool. Rhett had told her to make herself at home, and that's exactly what she'd done. He'd mentioned that he had a few things he needed to wrap up at his office in town, and then he wanted to stop by the police department to check on how things were going with his brothers. He told her that it might take a couple of hours and that he'd check in if he was going to be later. So far, he'd only been gone for forty-five minutes, but it seemed like forever.

She set her cell on a small table and stared out at the stars that appeared in the night sky. It was hard to believe that Rhett owned this magnificent piece of property. When he told her that he'd bought a house on the river, she hadn't expected it to be a little over three thousand square feet with a hundred and ten feet of water frontage.

Not to mention, the inside of the house had been completely remodeled with a beach-modern feel and had state-of-the-art everything.

Although, he could have used a female touch with some of the decorating.

The pool deck had a summer kitchen along with a tiki bar, deck, and a dock, and he had a thirty-foot center console fishing boat. He had kayaks, paddleboards, and everything else one would expect a man with a family to have on a piece of waterfront property.

Only, Rhett didn't have a family. She had to believe that he used this as a way to impress the women he dated.

And impress it would.

However, she'd been surprised that someone who worked as a private investigator could afford something so lavish.

He'd mentioned that being single and the fact that he saved his money helped, and, of course, he'd bought before the housing market went crazy, but still, this place must have cost a pretty penny.

Country music played softly from the speakers. He'd told her that his neighbors never complained about him being noisy, and he always had something piping through the sound system, whether it be music or the television. But she didn't want to be a pest, so she made sure to keep the volume down. But she couldn't stand silence. That would mean she had to think.

And that was the last thing she wanted to do.

Of course, her mind still went a million miles an hour. It would have been worse if she didn't have a song to focus on.

She didn't want to believe that her brother was using again, but that was the only thing that made sense. Except Jackie wasn't a drug addict. Other than the occasional glass of wine, she was about as straight as they came. She was sweet, kind, and generous. She could be a bit quiet, but she was good for Chris, and she loved him. That certainly showed.

Ties to the mob.

Those words kept coming back into her mind. It didn't make sense. And yet, maybe it did, because Chris and Jackie were missing. Perhaps Shelby had brushed off her concerns too quickly.

But she had trusted her brother. As she should.

Her therapist had told her that she needed to let Chris live his life. Make his own choices. He was a grown-ass adult, and Shelby had let her life suffer because she'd chosen—*chosen* being the keyword—to be the caretaker of her family. She didn't have to be that person anymore.

However, there were too many questions.

Things like: Why did they leave all their shit behind, including Chris's wallet?

And why the hell did they have a counterfeit one-hundred-dollar bill?

Shelby sipped her wine as her mind grappled for answers, but all she came up with were more questions. She inhaled sharply, letting the warm air fill her lungs. She closed her eyes and exhaled. One of her favorite songs came on, and she sang the words along with the band. She was tone deaf, so it was more of a whisper rather than her belting it out. She didn't want to scare the neighbors or the wildlife in case anyone was around. But she really needed to shut off the loop that kept replaying in her brain.

Her phone buzzed. She glanced at the vibrating device, expecting to see Rhett's contact information flash across the screen. Instead, it said *wireless caller.* She had no idea what that meant, so she let it go to voicemail, figuring it was probably a telemarketer. She'd been getting a lot of those calls lately.

Less than a minute later, her cell rang again.

She sighed as she reached for it, tapping the green button and putting it on speaker. "Hello?"

"Shelby?" Her brother's voice echoed in the night. "Are you alone?"

She bolted to an upright position, spilling red wine all over her tan pants. "Chris? Holy hell. Where are you? Are you and Jackie okay?"

"Answer my question," Chris said in a dark, commanding voice.

"Yes. I'm alone." She swung her legs to the side and set her glass on the table, ignoring her wet legs. "What's going on? I've been so worried about you."

"I'm sorry about that," he said. "I don't have much time, so listen carefully."

"You're scaring me." Her chest burned. Her eyes were like sandpaper, and she probably couldn't even shed a tear if she tried. Fear gripped her muscles. "The police found counterfeit money in your room. What was that all about?"

"I don't have time to explain. But it's not what you're imagining."

"I don't know *what* to think," she said. "I mean, are you involved with that Florida mob family, the

Mortellis, or something? I know you explained that, but now I can't help but wonder."

"Did the police find a key?" Chris asked, ignoring her question.

"What are you talking about?"

"Shelby," her brother said in a calm but harsh tone. "Just answer my question."

"No one said anything to me about a key."

"I need to know if they found a key. They should have it, but if they don't, I need you to get it."

"Where was it?" She stood and paced near the edge of the pool's deep end. Blue lights illuminated the water, and a warm breeze rippled across the top.

"In Jackie's jewelry bag. It was in a separate zippered compartment at the bottom in a pouch. It looks like a necklace."

Shelby blew out a puff of air. "Why didn't you take it with you? And what is it for?"

"I didn't have time," her brother said. "I barely had time to grab my keys and climb out the window."

"Excuse me?" She paused and glanced at the bright moon hanging in the dark sky. It was white and nearly full. It stared back at her, almost mocking her. "Why did you have to do that?"

"I can't get into all the details right now, but someone is after me and Jackie. That necklace literally holds the key to our freedom. If the bad guys got it, we're fucked. If the cops have it, we could still be screwed."

"That's not true. The cops here are brothers of a friend of mine."

"I saw you there," Chris said.

"How is that possible? And do you know who called me? Because the hotel manager—"

"You ask too many questions," Chris said. "I don't know if I can trust you. But I need help."

"I can't believe you just said that. Of course, you can trust me." She pursed her lips and held in her anger. Chris was the only family she had left in the world. She would do almost anything to protect him and keep him safe. "Tell me what's going on. I've heard the rumors about Jackie's uncle. Are they true?"

"Are you still in Lighthouse Cove?" Chris asked, still dodging her question.

"Yes," she said softly, her mind filling with even more questions.

"Are you willing to keep this phone call a secret from Rhett and his cop family for a little while?"

She froze. She'd never mentioned Rhett's name to her brother. Not in the past, and not in this conversation. "How do you know my friend's name?"

"That's not important right now. I need you to stay focused. Can you keep a secret from him?"

She closed her eyes for a long moment. Her heart jumped to the back of her throat before bottoming out in the pit of her gut. Rhett was doing her a huge favor by looking into her brother's disappearance—something he didn't have to do. Along with offering her a free place to stay, which really helped since she didn't have much money. Her father had left her with a lot of debt when he died, and before that, she'd taken care of whatever bills his insurance didn't pay, which was a lot. She was living paycheck to paycheck, and in order to come down to Lighthouse Cove to look for her brother, she'd had to take unpaid time off.

"I need you to answer a question for me without getting mad." She blinked open her eyes.

"I'm not using." His voice came across the speaker, loud and clear.

She believed him one hundred percent.

"Okay. I won't say a word."

"Good," her brother said. "Find a way to get our things. Go through them. If you don't see the key, you can ask if they took it. Or you can make up a story about it being a family piece of jewelry."

"I'll figure something out." Five years ago, she'd kept a lot of information from Rhett while in close quarters.

She suspected she could do it again.

"How can I get ahold of you? There was no number attached to this call."

"You can't. I'll be in touch. Please be careful." The phone went dead. The music seemed louder. A boat engine hummed in the background. Her heart hammered between her ears. She swallowed slowly. It hurt. It was as if her throat could no longer perform the simple task.

She became aware of the dampness on her thighs and the dryness of her mouth.

Time to change her clothes, get some more wine, and work on a way to bring up the topic of her brother's belongings. She had a right to them, especially if they weren't evidence. But she couldn't sound defensive. And if she came off as desperate, Rhett would know that she was looking for something.

She should have stayed at a hotel and not taken Rhett up on his random act of kindness. Only that was a double-edged sword because if she hadn't accepted, she wouldn't be so close to him, giving her the opportunity to ask him questions and request Jackie's and Chris's stuff.

She needed to learn to walk this fine line and use it to her advantage so she could help her brother and his girlfriend out of whatever trouble they'd gotten themselves into without tipping off Rhett and his cop family.

Rhett stepped outside and inhaled sharply. The thick stench of his lie filled his lungs. Pangs of guilt soured his belly. He should have told Shelby that he was going back to the hotel. But what was done was done.

"What are you thinking, big brother?" Emmerson asked.

Rhett laughed. They were barely a year apart. Sometimes, he wondered if his parents had kept having babies so they wouldn't get divorced given their marriage hadn't been very good. It wasn't until Jamison, the seventh child, came around that they'd stopped having more kids. And he wasn't even their father's child biologically. Of course, they'd also given up on having a girl.

Thank God.

Rhett didn't think they'd know what to do with one, and she'd get teased to no end and not just by the brothers.

"We know someone left the window open," Rhett said. "The clerk mentioned that the couple checked in at three in the afternoon and said they never saw them after that."

"They don't have security cameras here, but so far, no one that I questioned remembers seeing the vehicle Chris drives except for that first day. And it was parked right outside of his room." Emmerson rubbed the back of his neck—a tell that every single one of his brothers had when something bothered them. It was as if they were trying to rub the answers to the surface.

But it never worked.

"What about Chris and Jackie? Anyone remember them?"

"Only the clerk. And no remembers anyone else coming or going from this room," Emmerson said.

"I find it strange that the window in the bathroom was open. If whoever was chasing them ransacked this place after they chased them off, I would think they would have closed the window to make it look more like they went missing. Along with taking the wallet. That was a big mistake."

"Unless they had company and had to climb through the window themselves." Emmerson pointed to the big picture window by the door. "That one doesn't open. But clearly the one in the bathroom does. If the curtain was drawn, and they saw someone coming from the office right before we got here, maybe like the manager, who might have had Chris's sister tagging along? They might have hauled ass."

Rhett furrowed his brow. "There are fifteen rooms, six cabins, and limited parking. Where was their car?"

"My best guess is that they parked on the back side of Route 1. Or maybe in the parking lot of the drugstore. They could have hopped the fence easily and acted as if they were going for a stroll like everyone else."

Rhett had to admit that's what he would have done. "If Chris was smart, he would have moved his car in the middle of the night, especially if he believed that someone was coming for him."

Emmerson strolled to his patrol vehicle and

leaned against the hood. "Why Lighthouse Cove of all places?"

Rhett had already been rolling that question around in his brain. He stood a few feet from his brother and scanned the area. The hotel was on the outskirts of town, closer to Rottana Beach, which wasn't the nicest area but still within Lighthouse Cove's jurisdiction. However, one street over, and it became someone else's problem. That would have made this a whole different ball game.

At least this put it in his mother's wheelhouse.

"Shelby said her brother didn't know about me, and while Lighthouse Cove is a nice little beach town that most people wouldn't think about and could be a good hiding place, it's too much of a coincidence."

"You feel like he brought all this to our doorstep," Emmerson said.

Rhett nodded. "He also checked in using a credit card. That's traceable. It's like he wanted us to know he was here. And not just any law enforcement. The Kirby family."

"What about their place of employment? What do they say about their disappearance?"

Rhett rubbed the side of his face. "Shelby was told that her brother and Jackie took a vacation with her uncle, which I find odd because I believe her brother would have mentioned it. She called the officer that she filed the report with to give him the information. I believe that squelched the missing persons case."

"She was probably seen as an overprotective, overbearing sister," Emmerson said. "I've seen one or two of those in my day, and while Mom won't let us brush them off, it's hard not to because, half the time, whoever is missing is simply looking for a little time and space."

"I get that." Rhett had seen it, too, especially in cases like these. But Shelby had mentioned more than once that she hadn't been worried about her brother at all except for a brief time after their father's death.

And then these last several weeks. And only based on behavior.

What he needed to do was look at her phone and read the text exchanges between her and Chris without making it seem too weird. It wasn't that he didn't believe everything she'd told him, because he did. Still, he needed to gain a better understanding of the relationship.

"I have to admit, the counterfeit bill was pretty fucking good, except for the fact that we'd already seen a few pass through the marina this week. It's one of the reasons Mom has been in an uproar over this possible connection to the Mortellis."

Rhett arched a brow. "Why is this the first I'm hearing of that?"

"Mom wasn't sure she even wanted you to know," Emmerson said. "She sent the bills to the state crime lab, but initial comparison shows they are from the same print run, which means the bill Chris was carrying came from whoever handed it off at the marina."

"And you have no idea who that was?"

"We have a lead," Emmerson said. "Cole Laurita is back in town. He has a slip at the marina, and we've got him on security surveillance footage with packages being transported on and off his boat. But we can't put him with the counterfeit money that came into the marina. Not yet, anyway."

"Shit. How's Mom with Cole being back?"

"She's constantly rubbing her lower back where he shot her, but other than that, she seems fine. Dad asked me to keep an eye on her. He's always been concerned about when Cole got out."

"We should be worried about Dad and what he might do." Rhett said. "They might not be married anymore, and they probably should have gotten divorced long before Jamison was born, but you know how Dad gets when he feels like his family—and he considers Mom part of that—has been threatened."

"I know. Seth's keeping a watchful eye, so we've got all bases covered," Emmerson said. "Thing is, we all have a bone to pick with Cole Laurita, but he's not worth any of us getting ourselves in hot water over."

His brother had a point. "How were the bills not checked?" Rhett brought his thought back to the current case. Most places taught their employees to check larger bills, and it wasn't that hard. But these bills were well done. A teenager might not notice the difference, but they should have gotten a manager.

"Good question. I don't have an answer. Mom and Emmett are taking lead on things with the marina. I've got this situation."

"I'm sure you're all looking forward to when Nathan comes back from vacation." Rhett knew how hard it was on his brothers and his mom when one of them took even a day off. It wasn't easy being a small-town police department mostly made up of family, but they made it work.

"Mom keeps putting off setting a wedding date because there's no way in hell we can all take time off together."

"She and Steve should just elope," Rhett said. "Or she should retire."

"We are hiring, so that should help." Emmerson pushed from the hood of his vehicle. "We need to clean up that room. I have no reason to keep it. But something tells me we're missing a clue. Do you mind bringing that stuff back to your friend and going through it with her?"

"Not at all. I only wish we had found something useful."

"You and me both," Emmerson said. "I'm glad she's staying with you. How long do you think that will last?"

"I don't know. I can't force her to stay, but I'm thinking if we don't find him, it'll be three or four days at most before she gets antsy. Unless we get some good leads," Rhett said. "Any chance this counterfeit money and Cole are attached to the drugs washing up on the beaches?"

"That's what Mom thinks. But if that's the case, it could bring all this back to Chris and Jackie, and that's not going to be good for your friend."

Rhett didn't like the sound of that because it

meant that Shelby's brother could be using again, when it sounded more like he'd been on the run from something nefarious. Rhett would prefer it to be the latter, at least for Shelby's sake. Rhett knew how much she loved her brother and wanted Chris to be healthy and happy.

"You look like you're either constipated or stepped in dog shit," Emmerson said, waving his hand in the air. "No one believes Shelby has anything to do with this."

"But you all think Chris and Jackie do."

"No one is saying that. Right now, we have a hotel room with all their shit left behind. And counterfeit money that might be tied to a known drug dealer who's recently been let out of prison." Emmerson waggled his finger. "We still need to find out who he had contact with while he was locked up."

"But Jackie's family is potentially tied to the mob."

"Her uncle had a connection to the Mortelli family twenty-seven years ago and is now rumored to have more, but that doesn't feel right to me either. It also doesn't mean that Jackie is involved at all." Emmerson lowered his chin. "Don't go looking for trouble where it doesn't exist."

"This, coming from my cop brother."

Emmerson chuckled. "We have no reason to believe anything. All we know is that Chris and Jackie are missing. Now, as far as the counterfeit money goes… We're all willing to give them the benefit of the doubt. For now. At least until we find them. Or find more answers. So, let's go find them."

Rhett was down with that. "Is there anything in that hotel room you want to keep?"

Emmerson glanced at the sky.

"What is it?" Rhett knew that look, and he didn't like it.

"While you were outside talking with Shelby, we got an anonymous tip that there might be a key on a necklace in a jewelry bag that has some significance."

"Are you fucking kidding me? Were you not going to tell me?" Rhett asked. "Jesus. We've been standing out here discussing all this, and you're just telling me *now*? What the fuck, man?"

"Don't go getting your panties in a wad," Emmerson said with an arched brow. "And you better not tell Mom I'm filling you in. This is one of those things where what we do and what you do are in constant conflict. If she finds out, she'll pretend to take my badge for five minutes. I fucking hate it when she does that. I'm not a child."

Rhett couldn't relate to the badge thing, but he totally got the rest. "That's fair. What do you think the key is for or to?"

"It looks like it could be to a safety deposit box. We're going to check it out," Emmerson said. "But if anything else resonates with Shelby, I want to know about it."

"Copy that. Just don't keep shit from me anymore. I'm knee-deep in this, and I'm not going anywhere." Rhett turned on his heels and headed back toward the room. He and his brother made a list of everything, copied it, and texted it to their mom. Now, all he had to do was collect it and put it in his Jeep. It wasn't much, but he knew it would mean something to Shelby. Maybe she could make sense of something.

4

As quietly as he could, Rhett tiptoed into his family room. He'd decided he would bring all of Chris's and Jackie's things in tomorrow morning. It was too risky to do it now. Shelby could be awake, or he could make too much noise, knowing she tended to be a light sleeper.

And then he'd have to explain why he had her brother's and Jackie's things, and Shelby would want to go through them immediately. He knew that about her, and all Rhett wanted to do was get a few hours of shut-eye.

Or at least try.

He'd put her in the guest room closest to the master. The pool guest room, which was on the other side of the house, was the nicest, but he thought being near her would help him sleep better. However, as he eased past her bedroom door, he realized that he'd likely be up all night thinking about what might have been.

"Rhett? Is that you?" Her voice filled the space between his ears like ice cream melting over the side of a cone on a hot summer's day.

"Yeah." He paused, noticing that the door to her room wasn't closed all the way, and an inch of light illuminated the crack. "Can I come in?"

Shit. What was he thinking asking to enter her bedroom at one in the morning? She was probably sitting on her bed in some skimpy little nightgown, reading a book.

Sexiest vision he could have imagined.

"Sure," she said.

He stepped over the threshold, and his knees buckled. There she was, sprawled across the comforter in one of his shirts.

Only one of his shirts.

With her ankles crossed and a magazine tossed to the side.

He made his way to the edge of the bed and sat. He should bolt to a cold shower, but instead, he rested his hand on her bare thigh, igniting a flame deep in the pit of his gut. "How are you holding up?"

"Obviously, I can't sleep."

He ran his hand up and down her sweet, silky skin. He wanted to comfort her and take all her worry away, storing it in his muscles so she didn't have to carry the burden.

As he'd done in Key West.

Only he hadn't known he'd been doing that. Well, he had. He just hadn't known what he'd been washing away from her soul.

"I know you're worried about your brother. I am, too. But please know I'm doing everything I can think of to find him."

"Did you come up with anything today? Any clues?" She let out a sigh.

He climbed into the bed and looped his arm around her, squeezing her shoulder.

She dropped her head, snuggling against his chest.

Just like she'd done every night five years ago. She fit next to his body like the perfect golf glove.

"Not yet. However, I struggle with the idea that your brother just landed in Lighthouse Cove. Are you sure he had no idea about me?"

"I honestly don't know how he could have,"

Shelby said. "When he came home from rehab, we focused on his recovery. I helped him get into a halfway house and find a job. And then it was the rules for him living with Daddy. Everything was about him. Or when my dad's cancer came back, it was all about that."

"Never about you." He ran his hands through her long, thick hair. It filled his heart with a world of hurt that she took care of everyone and moved mountains for those she loved, and no one did even the littlest things for her. "Always about everyone else in your life."

"You make it sound like no one cares about me."

"I didn't mean it that way," he said. "I'm sure your father and brother appreciated everything you did for them." He tilted her head. "I'm sure you're loved and valued. I don't mean to make it sound like they use you or anything like that."

"That's kind of how it came out."

"What I meant was that you don't do a lot of self-care. I noticed that about you in Key West. You struggled with me taking care of you and doing even small things for you."

"I'm just not used to it."

That statement saddened him to his core. It

hardened him in a way that hurt his heart. He didn't understand anyone who couldn't get used to having someone do nice things for them. The desire to be taken care of was human nature to him.

He wanted it.

He just didn't know how to be in a relationship with anyone other than…well, the woman that was in his arms.

When he loved, he loved with his entire being. He understood that it went too far with Krista and that he allowed his love for her to devour who he was as a man.

He'd never let Shelby do that.

But he also never gave them a chance to find out if they could be anything more than a memory.

"I wish you could be." He kissed her forehead. "You deserve the world."

"I appreciate you saying that."

He cupped her chin. "Do you hear yourself?"

"Excuse me?"

"You don't believe that you deserve someone to take care of you the same way you take care of everyone else."

Her lips parted, and she released a slight gasp.

He wanted to tell her about all the things she was worthy of and how she should be treated. That her world didn't need to revolve around her brother and his demons. That she needed to live her life.

But instead of letting the words rumble from his throat, he pressed his mouth over hers in a hot, passionate kiss. He half-expected her to push him away as she fisted her hand in his shirt. However, she pulled him closer, deepening the kiss.

He told himself that he'd pull away in a minute or two. That he'd only let this last for a moment. That all he needed was a taste to get him through the night.

However, he knew he'd have to rely on her to call it off. He didn't have the strength to end what he'd started. Not when his hand slipped under her shirt and curled over her hip. It took every ounce of energy he had to keep from sliding it up her back.

That control began to slip as she pressed her knee between his legs.

He groaned, hugging her tighter. His tongue twirled around hers like a raging hurricane crashing against the shore. Finding the clip of her bra, he unhooked it.

She straddled him, removing her top and tossing it to the side.

No one was as beautiful as Shelby. Nor was there anyone as sweet and kind. She was a unique individual, and Rhett was one hell of a lucky man to have been touched by her, even for such a short period of time. He didn't care that he hadn't known her deepest, darkest secrets.

He'd known enough to give her his heart five years ago, and even if he wanted to take it back, that was impossible. The most interesting thing to him about this had to be that he trusted her with it. A small part of him said he shouldn't. He didn't know if that was all the pains of the past or maybe a little fear of the future.

Needing to remove his clothing, he flipped her to her back. He hated separating their lips. As quickly as he could, he ripped off his shirt and wiggled out of his jeans. Before he had a chance to pull her back into his arms, she had her hands and lips on his stomach and was kissing her way south.

He sucked in a deep breath and piled her hair on the top of her head. He wanted to enjoy everything she had to offer. He didn't want to be in control. Letting her take charge of whatever they did became more important than them doing anything at all.

If she wanted to stop right now, that would be fine with him. All he cared about was that she had all her needs and wants met.

And that, for this moment in time, he had the power to wash away all her concerns—even if only for one night. He was more than willing to take breadcrumbs.

For now.

Somehow, when this was all over, he'd ask her about maybe doing this right. He knew that he should stop her right here and now and start this off on a different foot. That he should take things slow.

But this felt as if they were getting closure for five years ago while saying hello all at once.

Or maybe he was kidding himself.

Did it even matter at this point?

His breath stopped short when she took him into her mouth. The things she did with her tongue and the way she touched him drove him crazy. He could only handle so much of this before he had to stop her; otherwise, he would explode, and no way would he let that happen too soon. Not before he had a chance to hear his name roll off her sweet lips in the throes of desire.

"Up here." He tugged at her hair.

She licked her lips and smiled.

All the air in his lungs escaped like a bird flying into a perfectly clear window at full force.

He cupped the back of her neck and crushed her against his body. He kissed her so hard that he worried he'd bruise her lips. Turning her onto her back, he made his way down her neck, stopping at her breasts and taking some time with her tight, puckered nipples.

She arched.

This was the kind of woman he couldn't get enough of. She was stronger than she gave herself credit for. She loved deeply. She was loyal, and she never asked for a lot when it came to herself.

All he wanted was to please her and make her happy. He knew how to do that in the bedroom. He was confident there. But he wasn't sure how to carry that over into other areas. He didn't know enough about her real life, and that hurt his heart in unexpected ways. In general, he wasn't an overly selfish man; however, he found himself wanting to lock her up in this house and not let her go until they'd had the proper time to get to know each other.

But that was ridiculous thinking. That was the past catching up with his present. That was his mind reaching into the memories of Key West while he listened to her moan. He remembered exactly what made her body hum and was relentless in his touches.

She clutched her fingers in his hair, and her hips moved with his mouth. She whispered his name over and over again as her climax spilled onto his tongue.

The sudden desperation to fill her overcame him, and he couldn't squelch it. He climbed on top of her and thrust himself into her, hard and fast. Her heels slammed into the backs of his knees as her fingers dug into his shoulders.

He could only hope that he didn't hurt her as he continued to lose himself inside her in a way he'd never done before. It was almost as if he'd returned home from a long journey.

And she welcomed him with open arms.

"Rhett," she whispered, kissing his neck right under his earlobe. "Yes. Yes."

His orgasm exploded with so much power it made him dizzy. His breath caught in the center of his chest. It tightened, and for a moment, he couldn't breathe.

As he lay on top of her, a pang of guilt filled his soul. As much as he wanted to be with her, he shouldn't have climbed into her bed. He should have at least waited a few days before making a pass at her. It didn't matter that she'd accepted him easily.

She was hurting, and maybe all she was looking for was some kindness. He could have held her and given her comfort that way.

He rolled to the side, pulling the covers over their naked bodies. He couldn't take back what they'd done. And to be fair, he didn't regret it. There was real, raw emotion between the two of them. That hadn't changed.

But neither had the circumstances when it came to Shelby.

She draped her arm across his middle and kissed his chest. "Anyone ever tell you that you're really good at that?"

He chuckled. "You might have mentioned it the last time we were together." He pressed his lips to her temple. "But you're the one who brings it out in me."

She rolled, resting her chin on his chest. "Do you remember the first time we met?"

"Oh, yeah." He'd never forget. "I made a complete ass of myself by trying all my best lines on you, and you flat-out told me to try them on someone else."

"You turned your back on me and literally gave

it your best shot with some bimbo who slipped you her room key," Shelby said. "I couldn't believe it. She'd been sitting there listening to you hit on me for an hour and was all like, '*If she won't fuck you, I will.*' Well, no way was I letting you go off with that tramp."

He burst out laughing. "For the record, I never would have. She wasn't my type. But I also didn't expect you to shove your tongue down my throat five seconds later and drag me off to your room."

"Yeah. That was a bit unexpected and not something I would normally do."

"I got that impression." He brushed her hair back from her face. "I didn't plan on us being together when I walked into your bedroom tonight. It's obvious that we have a serious attraction for one another."

"There's no denying that," she said. "But I'm not ready for this."

"I get it." And he did. He understood her better than he wanted to admit.

"However, I don't want to be alone tonight, and I feel horrible asking you to stay."

"Don't. If I didn't want to be right here with you, I'd leave. But I want to be with you, so I'm not going anywhere." He rolled over and shut off the reading lap. "Now, close your eyes and try to get some sleep."

She snuggled in behind him, holding on tightly.

He let out a slow breath.

It would be a long night.

5

Shelby hated to admit that she'd slept like a freaking baby. Being with Rhett again hadn't just been sexually gratifying, it had been emotionally fulfilling. She cared for Rhett. More than any other man she'd ever been with.

If she were being honest, she'd fallen in love with him five years ago, and it appeared those feelings rose to her heart like a submarine charging to the surface of the sea.

When she woke up alone, her heart had frozen. She'd thought she might have dreamt the entire experience, but then she found a sticky note on the pillow with a smiley face. He'd always been so cute with things like that.

She padded from her room to the kitchen in

search of caffeine and maybe some toast. The second she opened the door, the scents of sizzling bacon and coffee assaulted her nose. And if she wasn't mistaken, French toast.

He remembered.

"Good morning," she managed as she approached the island in the middle of the room. She pulled up a stool and tried not to stare at Rhett as he flipped a piece of egg-soaked bread onto the griddle. He wore a dark T-shirt and a pair of jeans that hung low on his hips. He pretty much wore that every day.

Unless he was at the beach or near a pool.

He looked good in anything.

"Why didn't you wake me?" she asked.

"I figured you could use the sleep." He paused in what he was doing with the breakfast food to pour her some coffee. He put in a dash of sugar and a couple of drops of cream.

Amazing that he hadn't forgotten anything about her after five years. Most people would have. But not Rhett, and she wasn't sure where to store that in her brain.

Or her heart.

"Thanks." She lifted the mug and blew before

taking a small sip. She tried not to moan. "You didn't have to make this big of a spread."

He laughed. "I always enjoyed your appetite in the morning. I've never seen anyone eat as much as you."

"When I do that, I tend to graze the rest of the day. And, honestly, I don't eat like that on a regular basis. I usually just have some plain toast or a bagel. But I really appreciate you going to all this trouble."

He pushed a plate of French toast loaded with butter and syrup with a side of bacon in front of her. He snagged his own plate along with his coffee and joined her, sitting right next to her, their elbows practically touching. "No trouble at all. I'm a breakfast guy. Though it's usually an egg sandwich from a drive-thru."

"How the hell do you stay so fit when you eat fast food like that?"

He shrugged. "Good genes, I guess." He dug into his food and shoveled half of it into his mouth.

It smelled so good that she couldn't resist plopping a large bite into hers, as well. They sat in silence until they'd both finished their meals, and then he was on his feet, doing the dishes and pouring them both a second cup of his delicious brew.

She'd missed having someone in her life. She nearly choked on the thought because she'd never really had a long-term relationship worth speaking of.

She'd been taking care of her family for years. First, her mother's depression, which had started when Shelby and Chris were in grade school. It was so bad, she could barely get out of bed. And it got so bad that Shelby and Chris wouldn't bring their friends over. For Shelby, it wasn't that big of a deal. But for Chris, it really affected him, and that's when his drug use started.

By the time Shelby was a sophomore in high school, she'd become the family's caretaker.

When her father was diagnosed with cancer during her senior year, her mother died by suicide two weeks later.

Everything went downhill from there.

Chris took it personally. It was as if he'd done something wrong, and their mother had done this terrible thing to punish him. When, in reality, she'd simply wanted her pain to end.

Shelby had opted to go to community college and worked to help support the family. She'd given up her childhood, and she had no regrets. Or so she'd thought.

After meeting Rhett in Key West, she'd realized how resentful she'd become and how much she wanted her life back. Rhett not calling her in those first few weeks had tormented her, but she couldn't bring herself to pick up the phone. Because if her brother went off the deep end, she knew without a doubt that she'd once again dedicate her life to Chris.

Her therapist told her she was addicted to it, and this trip proved it.

Only this felt different. As much as she'd worried that her brother was using again, and some of his behavior *did* scream *addict*...

His voice. His facial expressions. His eyes, did not.

But she'd chosen to believe that he'd fallen off the wagon. That he'd gone back to his old ways. And instead of asking him what was going on, she'd treated him like a child. And now, he was in trouble.

"Either you are making love to that cup of coffee, or you are in some serious thought about something deeper than a bottomless pit." Rhett leaned across the counter and tapped her wrist.

She blew out a long breath. "Sorry."

"Care to share?"

Lifting her gaze, she swallowed. Hard. Let the

lies begin. Or maybe half-truths because Rhett didn't know about her mother. Not all of it, anyway. "I was just thinking about my mom."

"She passed away when you were in high school, right?"

"You have a wicked-good memory." That had been one of the few truths about her past she'd shared with him five years ago.

"Goes with the job," he said. "It's both a blessing and a curse. It drove my ex crazy because, when we fought, I tossed so much shit back at her it wasn't fair."

"Yeah. That's not nice." She waggled her finger. "If you ever do that to me, I'll hurt you."

"I'll remember that," he said. "So, what about your mom?"

She took a sip of courage while contemplating if she should be honest or not. By the time she swallowed, she'd decided that if she couldn't tell Rhett the truth right now, she'd never be able to get through these next few hours or days when it came to Chris. "My brother has always blamed himself for Mom's death. Even sometimes today, when he knows it's not his fault."

Rhett arched a brow. "You never told me how she died."

"You never asked." She groaned. That came out ass-backward.

He took a large gulp of his beverage and held her stare. "In Key West, I was trying not to get too deep, even though I was having pretty intense feelings for you."

Her heart got stuck between the center of her chest and her throat. It constricted her ability to take a deep breath.

Or respond.

"If I learned too much about your life—if I got close—well, you're the kind of girl I would have fallen for, and I didn't think that would have ended well considering my headspace. I didn't want to hurt you."

"I can relate to that concept." Nothing about her three weeks in Key West had been fair. Nothing about how her life had turned out had been just. But what was she to do about it? She'd made those choices, and she had to live with them. And now her brother needed her help. Again. That was what she needed to focus on.

"We're really good at not getting into the nitty-gritty," he said. "How did your mom die?"

"She took a bunch of pills."

"Jesus," he muttered. "That sucks."

"It was her choice. I'm a strong enough person to know it had nothing to do with me. Of course, I've been in therapy since I was eleven. By choice. My brother would never go, and my dad only went occasionally, though he always supported my decision."

"That's good," Rhett said. "Why wouldn't your brother go?"

"Because my mom was proud of him for being the strong one. She told him that therapy was for the weak and that only losers went."

"I'm sorry, but that's kind of fucked-up."

"I know. I tried to encourage him, especially after she died, but he wouldn't have it. Of course, he was hooked on cocaine before my mom passed, so his head wasn't even in the game."

"That's a rough life. And not just for him."

She couldn't agree more. Shelby worried about her brother much like she'd feared for her mom. It had been constant. "We hid my brother's drug use from my mom. My dad and I thought it would make things worse. When my dad was diagnosed with cancer the first time, I wanted to hide that from her, too, but that didn't happen, and that's when she took her life. But what I was thinking about just a bit ago was that after my brother got out of rehab, which was the first time he'd really given getting clean a try, the only big trigger he had in five years was my father's cancer and then his death."

"So, what you're saying is that you no longer believe he's on a bender?"

She needed Rhett to know that her brother was in trouble. That he needed help. But that he wasn't a criminal. She had no idea what the counterfeit money meant. Or where her brother had gotten it. And he hadn't addressed it. He'd only been focused on the key. The necklace.

Which she didn't understand. All she knew was that her brother needed it.

"I don't know. But I wasn't upfront with you about something." Lying didn't come easily, especially with someone she cared about. Sleeping with Rhett last night had only made this harder.

Rhett stood tall. "I'm listening."

"My brother took something from my house. Something that belonged to my mother. And I want to know if your mom and brothers will let me go through his stuff to see if it's there."

"You're in luck. It's all in my home office."

She jerked her head. "Why didn't you tell me last night?"

"Because we got a little preoccupied with other things, and it was one in the morning." He lifted his finger. "However, before we go through his stuff again—"

"What do you mean by *again*?"

He rubbed the back of his neck. "Obviously, I went back to the hotel since I have Chris's and Jackie's belongings. Before I brought it here, Emmerson and I went through it all."

"I should be really pissed at you for lying to me." My God. That was so uncalled for, but he didn't know her lie.

"You just told me you weren't totally honest either. So, let's call that one a wash," he said. "Now, what exactly are you looking for?"

"A necklace with a key attached to it." She didn't see any reason she couldn't tell Rhett what she was looking for since it was a simple piece of jewelry—or so she'd made it out to be. Lots of people had keys attached to jewelry. "My mom was wearing it when she died." God she hated lying. It left a bitter taste in her mouth. "It has sentimental value to both of us."

"Is it worth money?"

She couldn't say yes to that because if she found it and it looked cheap, Rhett would start asking a million questions. "It's always been a bone of contention between us. My mom promised it to Chris when he found the right girl, but he hasn't said that about Jackie. Yet. And I kept it because I couldn't trust him not to sell it for drugs when he was using."

"And you believe he was sneaking around your house for that necklace and your mom's wedding rings?"

Interesting that Rhett chose to toss in the rings when she had only mentioned that Chris had tried to steal them five years ago. "I don't keep them in the same place. The rings are in my safe, which is in my closet. I wear the necklace sometimes and keep it on my dresser in my bedroom. I don't know why or if he took the necklace for sure, but I just want to know if he did."

"You wearing it sometimes…isn't that kind of a slap in the face to your brother, if it's meant for his bride?"

She narrowed her eyes. Rhett's comment shouldn't sting since the entire story about the key and necklace was total bullshit. But the words hurt, nonetheless. "Until he marries. It's mine."

"I get it. I've got brothers. It might be a different dynamic than a sister, but we have our issues."

Rhett nodded. "We didn't see anything that fit that description, but let's go take a look."

"Thank you. I appreciate it." Her pulse pounded in her throat. She suspected that her heart rate was probably in the red zone. Once she went through her brother's shit, she'd find a reason to hit the road.

"No problem." Rhett reached across the counter and took her hand. "One more thing. Would you mind it if I looked at the text messages between you and your brother?"

"Why?" She remembered deleting the call last night, which meant that Rhett wouldn't be able to tell she'd spoken to anyone. But that didn't make her feel any better. Not that she had intense deep conversations with her brother, but they were private and personal and none of Rhett's business.

Then again, her brother was in trouble.

"A different set of eyes might give us a different perspective on his frame of mind the last few weeks before his disappearance. I might pick up on something that you didn't because you're too close."

She had to admit, that made sense. But she wanted to say no. She was too scared that her brother might call or text while Rhett had her phone. "Those messages are between brother and sister. I'd feel like I was breaking a confidence."

"I don't want to make you feel uncomfortable. Why don't you think about it while you go through his things?" He waved his hand. "Follow me. Everything is in my office."

She palmed her mug, hoping her hands didn't shake as she strolled down the hallway.

"I have to make some calls. Let me know if you find anything of interest." He pulled open a door.

She stepped into a small room with a desk strategically placed to face a sliding glass door that overlooked the river. "Wow. This is amazing." A colorful fish hung on the side wall. The back wall had a built-in bookshelf where he had pictures of him and his family, along with a couple of books.

Two suitcases and a couple of travel kits were on the floor.

Her missing brother's belongings.

She gasped.

He curled his fingers around her forearm. "Take your time. I'll be outside." He gave her a quick kiss, but it lacked the punch she expected from a man she'd just had sex with.

"Thank you." She dropped to the floor and ran her fingers over the top of the suitcase. She glanced over her shoulder as the door gently closed. "Chris. What have you gotten me involved in?"

Rhett jogged down the steps from his deck to his dock. He glanced over his shoulder. He couldn't see inside his office window, but he suspected that she was searching for the necklace that was currently in Emmerson's hands. Rhett sucked in a deep breath and let it out slowly. He needed to check his emotions.

Or toss them in the river.

It didn't help that he'd slept with her, which he didn't want to believe was a mistake.

He pulled his cell out of his back pocket and stared at it for a long time. He should call his mother, but he didn't feel like dealing with her first thing in the morning. "Hey, Siri. Call Emmerson." He climbed on his boat and sat in the bow, staring at the sun. He squinted since he hadn't brought out his sunglasses. He probably had a pair in the console, but he didn't feel like getting up off his lazy ass.

"What's up?" Emmerson answered on the second ring.

"She's lying," Rhett blurted out, his chest tightening. There were so many things he understood about Shelby and her motivations. He might have done the same if he were in her shoes.

But he wasn't.

He was here to help and support her. Last night should have changed things, but it hadn't. He had to accept that.

"Okay. About what?"

Rhett leaned back on the cushions and closed his eyes. He didn't deal with betrayal well, and to be lied to by someone he cared about hit him between the eyes. He should have anticipated it. Hell, he wasn't being truthful either. But that was because he couldn't. His brothers and their jobs prevented him from doing so.

He also had to put in perspective that she was, for all intents and purposes, a client, and they always withheld some truths. Those facts always came to light and, in general, his customers always realized they'd been stupid for keeping secrets.

"She knows about the necklace," Rhett said.

"As in we have it?"

"No. She's going through his things right now, looking for it," Rhett said.

"Why is that strange?"

"Because she told me yesterday that his behavior was off and that she caught him sneaking around her place. She mentioned that he'd tried to steal their mother's rings five years ago. Not a necklace with a key. But this morning, she suddenly tells me that her brother *did* take something. After she specifically said that nothing had been missing."

"It's not uncommon for people to do that, and you know it," Emmerson said.

Rhett chose to ignore his brother's comment. "I asked her if I could look at the text messages between her and her brother, but she said she feels like that might be breaking his confidence. I think she's been in contact with him. Or, at the very least, he called her last night and asked her to look for that piece of jewelry."

"That's interesting. Did you confront her?"

"No. Not yet, anyway. I'm playing it cool. I want to give her the opportunity to come clean and you some time to figure out where the key belongs. Is there any way it could be a family heirloom of some kind?"

"Sorry, man. I got confirmation about fifteen minutes ago that the numbers on the key match that of a bank not far from here."

"Shit," Rhett mumbled. "When are you headed there?"

"As soon as we can get the judge to sign a warrant. And we don't have much to go on. We're going to try to do it without Shelby confirming anything, but we could come knocking."

"That's fair. However, keeping her in the dark might work to our advantage. I'd like to find out what's in there without her knowing." Rhett closed his eyes and inhaled the salty air. It soothed his pounding temples. "What else do you have going on?"

"Not much," Emmerson said. "We have no leads other than this bank and Chris and Jackie. We're going to keep working on it, but outside of that, nothing. I've got other cases, and I'll be out on patrol. Is there anything you want me to work on or look for?"

"I don't know." Rhett pinched the bridge of his nose. "If I think of anything, I'll text you."

"Work on gaining her trust and getting her cell. She's scared. And if her brother is messed up in something, he's likely manipulating her. If he's being forced to do something, then he's running scared, and that key could be what he needs for his freedom."

"I know. I've thought of all of that, but I can't help her unless she's honest with me."

"So find a way to get her to do that," Emmerson said. "I've got to run. I'll talk to you soon."

Rhett set his cell on the seat and groaned. He'd loved Krista, and all she did was rip his heart to shreds. Then he'd fallen in love with Shelby but had chosen to protect his heart and let her drive away. He'd deleted her contact information and did his best to forget all about her so history didn't repeat itself. He'd thought he'd done the right thing for both himself and Shelby. At the time, he didn't believe that he was a whole man. He'd thought he couldn't completely give himself to a woman. By the time he'd figured out that he was ready, it had been two years, and he didn't have it in him to chase her down.

He'd never forgotten her, though, and the second he'd laid eyes on her, he'd been catapulted back to Key West, and his entire being burned with love. He couldn't shake it if he tried. It had been living inside him all this time, waiting to be released.

Maybe he wouldn't feel this way if he hadn't slept with her last night. But he had, and he couldn't change that fact.

And now she was lying to him when he was the only person who could help her.

Well, him and his family.

He certainly knew how to pick them.

When his parents finally divorced, which had honestly been a good thing, his mom had told him that love came in different shapes and sizes. That she loved his father, always had and always would, but that it wasn't a sustainable kind of love. She said that she'd known it when they got married, which meant she shouldn't have married him. She'd told Rhett that the love between a man and a woman should be something you couldn't put in words; however, you should see it as clear as day. And when two people experienced that emotion, it was like an explosion.

Rhett had asked her why she'd stayed with their dad, and she'd told him that when they had Seth, his eldest brother, she'd seen a kind of love that was so pure, it made her want more.

And that was the love between mother and child. And Dalton, Rhett's father, was the kind of man—at least, according to Rhett's mom—that not only loved with his entire soul but captured the essence of a person's heart. She'd told him that she'd stayed so long with his dad because he was the best father any child could ever ask for.

And she was right.

Only his mom had screwed up royally when she'd had an affair that'd created his baby brother, Jamison. When the truth came out, it'd nearly destroyed his family, and Jamison had had to deal with the fact that he wasn't Dalton's biological son. However, the love that Dalton had for Jamison had never wavered. Not a smidge. It'd taken time for Jamison to accept his biological father, Steve, but he eventually did.

Everyone welcomed Steve into their lives—in part because they had to. He wasn't going anywhere. Their mother had made that clear.

But when Steve and his mom walked into a room, their love for each other was palpable. He couldn't put what he felt into words, and he knew that Steve would never leave his mother's side again. That their kind of love was what fairy tales were made of.

He knew that was what he felt for Shelby.

And, right now, that sucked. He couldn't turn his emotions on and off.

His cell buzzed. He glanced at the screen and chuckled. It was as if his mom had a sixth sense.

"Hey, Mother."

"I hate it when you call me that. It sounds like you're pissed at me or something."

"Sorry," he said. "How are you this morning?"

"A little concerned about you."

He pushed himself to a sitting position and crossed his ankles. A few kayakers paddled by. He smiled and waved. This had to be his favorite part about living on the water—the peacefulness of it all and the way it calmed his nerves. Just sitting in this spot on his boat gave him the ability to focus.

Somewhat.

"And why is that?" he asked.

"I know you have feelings for this woman, but I'm not sure what to believe in this case."

"Neither do I," he admitted. "She's going through Chris's and Jackie's things. I'm going to have her go through his texts with me later and see if I can gain a different perspective on where his head was at. From there, I'm going to probe into what she knows about Jackie. I might even suggest a trip to Jacksonville."

"I don't think I want you doing that," his mom said.

"Why not?"

"I want you to keep her here for now. At least,

until I can get that warrant, which isn't going to happen until after banking hours today."

"Again, I ask. Why not?" He chuckled. It seemed that was the go-to question with his mom.

"The judge we want has a full docket today, and I don't want to push my luck with her. This warrant is thin, and if it were me sitting on that bench, I might say no."

"That's fair."

"So, I need you to find a way to keep Shelby in town for at least another twenty-four hours."

He rubbed his forehead. "That shouldn't be that hard."

"There's more," his mom said. "I believe this counterfeit money is connected to Cole Laurita and the drugs that washed up on the Lighthouse Cove beach."

A dull ache formed in the back of his skull and moved across his head. "Why do you think that?" It was kind of a dumb question because no one in his family, not even his full-time mechanic and part-time private investigator brother, Miles, believed in coincidences. And there were too many of those for all of it *not* to be connected.

"Preliminary labs on the counterfeit money show it was made on the same paper. The state lab believes the ink is the same. They have more tests to run, but I'm confident it came from the same place." She let out an audible breath. "How the hell does a guy who drives a limousine in Jacksonville get the same counterfeit money as a known drug dealer living in Lighthouse Cove?"

"That's a head-scratcher, Ma." He understood that his mother wasn't looking for him to pull a theory out of his ass. They didn't know enough about Chris, which was the next step.

A total deep-dive, and it wasn't going to make things easy with Shelby. He would have to ask some tough questions. Dig in some dark places. And not just in Chris's life but also in Jackie's and how it all tied into Shelby's, as well.

"Just keep her close and do what you do best."

"Yes, ma'am."

"Stay in touch," his mother said. "I love you."

"Love you, too." He tapped his phone and jumped to his feet. Time to turn up the charm and swallow his feelings. He had a job to do, and if there was one thing anyone could say about him, it was that he was a damn good private investigator.

6

Shelby made her way back to the kitchen after going through her brother's and Jackie's things—twice—and finding nothing of interest. No necklace or key. But she also spent her time thinking about Rhett and how he was doing so much for her, and she was doing nothing but betraying his trust.

She kept telling herself that she had no choice. She was doing it for her brother. To keep him safe, because he needed that. Because he'd asked that of her, and she was only being a good sister.

She checked her back pocket, making sure her cell was there. She'd put it on vibrate mode earlier so that if her brother called, she'd feel it instead of it ringing so she could lie and step out of the room if Rhett were nearby.

"Hey, you," Rhett said as he stepped through the sliding glass doors. "Did you find what you were looking for?"

"No." She rinsed out her mug and put it in the dishwasher, doing her best to keep her emotions buried deep in her gut. Part of her wanted to tell Rhett what was going on, but Chris had asked her not to, and since he'd sounded clearheaded, she had to trust him.

She absolutely believed that he wasn't using. She could hear that in his voice. That was a plus.

"He must have it with him," she said, hoping her voice didn't shake like her insides.

"Why is this piece of jewelry so important to you right now?"

Shit. This would be harder than she'd thought. She'd never been the kind of person who could think quick on her feet. It was why she'd chosen a profession where she didn't have to be around people. Sitting behind a desk and staring at a computer screen all day, inputting data, was better than having to deal with the general public.

She opened her mouth but then her cell buzzed. She pulled it out, and her heart raced. "This is work. I need to take it. Will you excuse me for a second?"

"Sure thing."

She raced across the house and into her room, shutting the door. "Hello?"

"Are you alone?" Chris asked.

"I am now," she said with a shaky voice.

"Should we hang up?"

"No. We're good." She paced at the edge of her unmade bed with her phone pressed hard against her ear. "I can't do this for much longer."

"Did you find the key?"

"It wasn't in your stuff."

"Do the cops have it? Or does Rhett?"

As quietly as she could, she opened the door and peeked out into the hallway. "Rhett says no, and he has no reason to lie to me."

"Are you sure about that?"

She closed the door gently. "He wants to help. And, right now, he and his family are looking for you."

"I don't want to be found," Chris said. "Not yet, anyway."

"Why? Tell me what the hell is going on."

"I can't. You have to trust me. The less you know, the safer you are."

"No. I don't believe that. Knowledge is power. Besides, Rhett and his family could keep you and Jackie protected from whatever you're running from."

"Maybe Rhett, but his mom is the chief of police. Right now, she'd be a dangerous person for me to be around, and I'm not going to get into why. I just need you to trust me."

"I trust Rhett," she said firmly. "You can, too. Please. He's in the kitchen. Let me go get him, and you can talk to him about whatever's going on. I'm begging you."

"I'm stuck between a rock and a hard place, sis." Her brother's voice was laced with thick emotion. "His family is duty-bound to bring me in for questioning, I'm sure of it. However, I do believe he'll take care of you."

"Duty-bound based on what? The counterfeit bill in your room? Even they said that doesn't necessarily mean anything. You could have gotten that anywhere, right?"

"But I didn't. And bad people are after me and Jackie. Right now, the cops are not my friends. I wish they were, but they're not. I need to know where that key is."

"Do you want me to ask Rhett flat-out? Because I have no problem doing that."

Chris let out a nervous laugh. "No. That's not going to help me. To be honest, if the bad guys have the key, I'll know by the end of the day."

"And then what?"

"I'll come to Rhett's place. Because then I'll really need his protection."

"Give me a time so I know when to freak out, and he'll know when to expect you."

"If you don't hear from me, or if I'm not there by seven, you can tell him everything. Text me the address at the number I'm about to text you. Then delete the string. You can keep the number as long as you put it in your contacts as something else. Someone that he won't know—or suspect."

"He wants to look at the messages between us."

"Let him."

"But I just told him this was a call from work. I can't delete it."

"Shit," Chris said. "Okay. Tell me a number from work, and I'll call you right back."

"You can do that?" She plopped down on the edge of the bed and pinched the bridge of her nose.

"Yes, now hurry."

"904-561-7563."

The phone went dead. Two seconds later, it vibrated in her hands.

"Hey," she said softly, surprised that it came over as a work line.

"We should stay on the line for a few minutes," Chris said. "Delete the other call. You can text me the address on this number but remember to delete that text."

"I'll do that now." Quickly, she sent him the pin to her location. Once she saw that it was delivered and read, she deleted it. "This is so crazy, Chris. Why is this happening?"

"We'll talk more tonight. I promise."

"Where are you?"

"Based on your location, I'm about forty minutes away."

She tried to take a deep breath but couldn't fill her lungs. She tapped her chest. She wasn't sure if that made her feel better or not. But it did make her feel somewhat connected to her brother, and that was something.

"I love you, Chris."

"I love you, too, sis." Once again, the cell went dead.

Tears stung the corners of her eyes. She sniffled and raced to the bathroom. Thank God his guest room had its own because she needed a moment before she faced Rhett.

She turned on the water and splashed some on her face. Leaning against the counter, she stared at herself in the mirror. All she had to do was hold onto the lies for a few more hours. If this wasn't all cleared up by seven, she could tell Rhett everything.

He might be mad for a little while, but he'd eventually understand.

Or maybe he wouldn't.

She was only doing what she had to for her brother. For family.

No one could fault her for that.

She squared her shoulders and headed back out to the kitchen where she found Rhett sitting at the counter, reading the paper as if he didn't have a care in the world.

"Is everything okay at work?" he asked, barely glancing over the top as he turned the page.

"Yeah. They just couldn't find my last report." Wow. She was becoming quite the little liar. "So, I was thinking about those messages from my brother, and I don't see any reason why you can't look at them." She placed her cell on the counter. "My passcode is 88521."

"Why the change of heart?" He folded the paper and set it aside.

"I think you're right. My opinion of my brother is skewed. I've been thinking about him and feeling a certain way for his entire life. It's not fair to him, or to me. Maybe you'll see something I couldn't."

Rhett arched a brow as if shocked. "What made you come to that conclusion?"

"Nothing and everything." She couldn't afford to continue blatantly lying to Rhett. It would eat her alive if she did. However, telling him the entire truth would only put her between a rock and a hard place with her brother, which would also destroy her. "I don't think he's using, but I think he's in trouble."

"Why?"

"Because none of this makes sense," she said. "He left his stuff behind. He has counterfeit money. He's not communicating with me. It doesn't add up."

"That's what happens when drug addicts pick up again."

"I know. That's what I thought because he was being so secretive. But the more I examine things, the more I believe he's not using. But something else *is* happening."

"All right. What exactly do you think the issue is?"

"I don't know," she admitted.

Rhett lifted her phone and tapped at the screen. "What can you tell me about Jackie?"

"She's a sweet girl," Shelby said. "Chris loves her. I don't know her as well as I'd like, but what I do know is that she's good for him."

"What about her family?" Rhett focused on her cell, scrolling with his index finger. He kept his gaze lowered, not lifting it at all. "What can you tell me about them? Her parents. Her siblings. Anything at all. It doesn't matter if you think the detail is immaterial; it might be the one thing that sends us down the right path."

"She doesn't have siblings. Her parents died when she was young. Murdered, actually."

"By whom?"

"All I know is it was unsolved. The police had no leads, though they suspected it was mob related. A family in New Jersey."

Rhett lifted his gaze. "That's a big statement. What can you tell me about that? Like, do you have a mob family name?"

"I think it was Gorga, but I'm not sure. Jackie blew it off as crazy-talk. Said that neither her uncle nor her father had any ties to either that mob family in New Jersey or the Florida one, and if the mob was involved, it wasn't…intentional," Shelby said for lack of a better word. "But it is why she and her uncle moved to Florida, to get away from all of that. To start fresh in a new town since the police had no suspects, and it became a cold case."

"Has she kept in touch with the police up north?"

"Not that I know of," Shelby said. "Her uncle raised her, and he's the one who owns the limo company." That's about all she knew about Jackie. In the last few weeks, she'd wanted to take Jackie out to lunch to get to know her better, but so many different things had gotten in the way.

Namely, the way her brother had been avoiding her and not returning her calls. It had been a difficult pill to swallow. While she didn't understand right now, she had a better feeling about why.

Sort of.

At least she knew it wasn't about her brother using drugs again. That somehow made this seem a little better in a weird way.

"Could his troubles, whatever they are, be related to Jackie?"

Her heart filled her chest with a painful pounding. Ever since her brother had gone missing, all she'd thought about were his past mistakes.

His drug use.

Ties to the mob.

Those rumors were few and far between. What little she'd uncovered was unsubstantiated and obviously wasn't huge news because she couldn't find too much information.

"I don't know," she whispered. The moment the three words flopped out of her mouth, she wished she could take them back because the last thing she wanted to do was stir up more problems. She didn't need Rhett calling his family and telling them that Jackie and her family could be the cause of anything.

Only, if they *were* connected, her brother could be in the kind of trouble that put people six feet under.

Shelby mentally rolled her eyes at herself. Rhett and his police brothers and mom had probably already given that some thought and most likely had done some research into Jackie's family themselves. Shelby was sure they knew more than she did.

"I'm so confused." She inhaled sharply. "I can barely keep it together. I'm really struggling. All I want is my brother back safe and sound and all this bullshit to be over." She felt the need to backtrack a little on how she'd initially approached Rhett. Not because she knew that Chris might be showing up on his doorstep but because she couldn't take lying anymore. "The only thing I know for sure is that my brother hasn't been acting like himself, and it all started when he took that job."

Rhett set her phone down. "When did he start dating Jackie?"

"About six or seven months ago." She thought being honest about that couldn't hurt. She ran through the conversation with her brother. Whoever was after him, if they had the key…oh, shit. There would be some kind of showdown between Chris and the bad guys at wherever the key led. That had to be why Chris had wanted her to hold off.

She bit down on her fingernail.

"What's going on?" Rhett reached across the counter and tugged on her hand. "Something is bothering you. And keeping it from me isn't going to help your brother."

"I don't know what to do."

"I can't help you if you don't tell me."

She closed her eyes, squeezing out a couple of tears. The only thing she had was a fake phone number. Maybe Chris would answer. Maybe he wouldn't.

If he did, the second he thought that something was off, he'd hang up, and he sure as shit wouldn't tell her where he was or what was going on.

And if he knew she'd broken his trust, he'd never speak to her again.

But what was worse, she could be putting him in even more danger.

However, if she did nothing… She shivered.

"Shelby. I know you've been lying to me. I've been doing my best to be patient, but something changed. If you know where your brother is, and if he's in trouble, I can help. But not unless you tell me what you know."

"I don't know much at all," she said through a sob. She leaned against the back counter and crossed one arm over her middle. She covered her mouth with her other hand and did her best to keep from all-out crying. The inside of her nose burned from keeping it all in.

Rhett closed the gap and wrapped his arms around her trembling body. He ran his hands up and down her back. He kissed her temple with his tender lips. "I know you're scared. I understand you want to protect your brother. I'd want to do exactly the same thing if I were in your shoes." He cupped her face and stared into her eyes. "You've got to trust that I only want to help. I'm here for you. I'm not going anywhere. Trust me."

She took in a slow, shallow breath through her nose and let it out through her lips. "Someone is after my brother."

"He told you that?" His hands moved from her back to her arms. He gripped them firmly but tenderly. There was nothing but kindness in his touch.

"He called me last night, asking about the key and the necklace. And again a little while ago. Since it's not with his stuff, and you don't have it, I believe he's going wherever that key fits to have a show-down with whoever is after him. And that isn't going to end well." She spoke so fast it felt as if her words smushed together like mashed potatoes. When she tried to pull in a long, slow, deep breath, the air stopped in the center of her chest and wouldn't fill her lungs. She coughed and tried again.

He took her chin with his thumb and forefinger. "Relax, Shelby, or you're going to work yourself into a full panic attack."

She blew out a puff of air and stared into his blue eyes. They reminded her of the Mediterranean ocean. Rich. Deep. And they drew her in, calming her nerves, making her feel safe and secure. She gripped his shoulders and focused on him and only him.

"That's it," he whispered.

"I'm so frightened for him."

"I know you are, but you don't have to be because we have the key."

"What?" She blinked. Her chest tightened. She had no right to feel the hot rage flowing through her bloodstream. "When did you find the key?"

"Last night."

"Before you came to my room? Before you made love to me?" Her blood turned into thick, hot tar.

He nodded.

She had half a mind to slap him, but that wouldn't do her any good. "Why didn't you tell me?"

"I couldn't," he said. "It's police business, and I wasn't allowed. It's a fine line for me to be doing it now."

"So you decided to have sex with me instead?"

"Seriously? We're going to have *that* fight right now, considering everything else?"

She clenched her jaw. He had a point. "Do you

know what the key opens? Because I don't, and Chris didn't tell me. He won't tell me where he is. He only made me promise that I wouldn't tell you anything unless he didn't call or show up here at seven tonight." Her lungs burned with every tiny little gasp of air she managed to suck in, and it wasn't enough to sustain her. "Is the mob after him? And if so, why?"

Rhett tilted his head. "Those are all questions that I and my family are trying to answer."

"It's all so confusing, and I'm scared."

"I know you are, but I can't protect you unless you're honest with me," Rhett said. "Did you give Chris my address?"

She nodded. "He told me if the bad guys had the key, he'd know by the end of the day. That tells me he's going to try to confront them or something."

"It sounds more like he's going to try to cut them off at the pass." Rhett brushed his lips across her cheek, letting them linger for a long moment before taking a step back. "This might be enough for my mom to interrupt the judge and get a warrant earlier."

"What are you talking about?"

"The key is to a local safety deposit box," Rhett

said. "But if we don't get the warrant, we can stake out the bank to find out who's after your brother." He rubbed the back of his neck. "Can you reach him?"

"I think so. I have a number. He did that thing where he creates a fake one."

"You can call that back."

"I doubt he'll answer it," she said.

Rhett snagged her cell and tucked it in his back pocket. "I need to call my mom before we do anything."

"What do you plan on doing?" Her pulse pounded in every muscle of her body. It vibrated through her system, creating a sense of panic that she couldn't shake.

"Not exactly sure because my mom will tie my hands a little. But the first thing will be to talk your brother into meeting me in the next hour or so."

Shelby turned. She didn't want him to see her completely lose it. Gripping the counter, she hung her head and inhaled sharply. She absolutely knew that the best thing would be for Chris and Jackie to, at the very least, meet with Rhett. "Is my brother going to be arrested?"

Strong arms came around her middle. Rhett rested his chin on her shoulder. "I can't answer that because I don't know if he did anything illegal. We're still researching all of this, but Joe Staub could have ties to the Mortelli family. I don't know how deep that connection goes, but it's something my mother is looking into. Add in what you told me about Jackie's parents being murdered, and it might have been connected to a mob family in New Jersey. I need you to tell me what you know so I can protect all of you."

She spun on her heels. "The Mortellis… Aren't they like drug dealers and shit?" A few months ago, she remembered seeing something on the news about one of the Mortelli boys and a drug bust. She couldn't remember the details, but the name had stuck in her head.

"They aren't good people." Rhett cupped her face. "I have more questions than I have answers, and I need you to promise me you're not going to lie to me anymore. I can't keep you safe or help your brother if you keep doing that."

She pursed her lips and narrowed her eyes. "Seems you've been keeping some things from me, too, so that sword swings both ways."

"That's fair. But there will be things I can't tell you. Even things my brothers and mom won't tell me. For now, you need to give me a minute to call

Emmerson and get the ball rolling. The longer we stand here and argue over this, the more your brother and his girlfriend could be in danger."

She nodded. "Okay. But I can't reach out to him when you have my phone."

"I don't want you to yet. We need a plan, and while I might be known for going rogue, I don't like to fly solo." He tilted his head and brushed his lips gently over hers in a sweet kiss. It wasn't overtly romantic, but it brought her back to five years ago. All the same emotions filled her soul, and she found herself leaning into him and soaking up his strength. "Do you trust me?"

"Yes," she whispered.

"Good." He strolled out of the kitchen, through the sliding glass doors, and to the outdoor patio.

Rhett had never been anything but kind to her, except when he hadn't called. But he'd explained that, and it made sense. As did why he'd chosen not to tell her about the necklace or anything else right away.

He didn't appear too pissed off about her lies.

She could only hope that she was doing the right thing for Chris.

7

    Rhett climbed up onto the captain's chair on his pool deck, holding Shelby's cell in his hand.

Shelby had brought out a bowl of grapes and a couple of bottled waters. He took one, twisted the cap, and chugged half, wishing it was straight tequila.

He'd spent twenty minutes on the phone with his mother and his brother, Emmerson. Ten of them were waiting for his mother to stop mumbling and swearing while she had someone else get ahold of the judge—which was the last thing she wanted to do. Especially when Rhett didn't want to bring Shelby into the mix by forcing her to sign anything to help the judge move the process along.

At the end of the day, Rhett didn't think they needed the warrant. Sure, he cared what was in the safety deposit box, but right now, he wanted Chris and Jackie front and center. If they were the ones that opened the box, they could get into it later.

"You don't look happy," Shelby said as she fiddled with her water. "I suppose that was kind of a stupid thing to say under the circumstances."

He wished he could shake the heavy weight from his shoulders when it came to Shelby, but he couldn't. His heart wanted him to pull her close and hold onto her forever, but his mind kept reminding him that she hadn't trusted him enough to be honest. And worse, he hadn't believed her. If he tried really hard to put himself in her shoes, he understood all the lies.

But that didn't make him feel better. She knew what he did for a living and that he could help.

He also worried that she wasn't being honest about her lack of knowledge regarding Jackie and her uncle's ties to the Mortelli family. Granted, he hadn't known; however, it hadn't taken but a single Google search for him to find the first article. It took some digging to get more, and he was good at his job. He knew which rocks to look under. People paid money to have certain things driven to the top of search engines, and other things buried.

Shelby was a smart girl. She knew how things worked. That said, on an initial search, Joe Staub was a guy from Jersey, who moved to Florida to start over after his brother and his brother's wife had been murdered.

One article mentioned that the murder could have been mob related and talked about the Staubs and their ties to the Gorga family. But that was it. Nothing substantial.

However, Rhett knew there was more. Especially when this kind of trouble followed the family to Florida.

"We don't have much time, so I'm going to send this text to your brother, but I want you to read it to make sure it sounds like you." He set the cell on the table and pushed it toward Shelby. His stomach soured. There were so many holes in this plan, which had been tossed together haphazardly, but they had to move fast. Emmerson had pushed their mother to either make it happen with the judge or turn a blind eye and let Rhett do whatever it took, knowing she wouldn't sit on the sidelines.

Not because she was that much of a control

freak, but because of all the connections with the counterfeit money.

But she never liked being pushed into doing things before she was ready or before she had her ducks in a row. She was a meticulous police officer, which was why she was the chief of police. She demanded perfection in her officers and expected nothing but the best from herself.

And her children, regardless of whether they were in law enforcement or not.

This particular sting operation had so many flaws that it made even Rhett itch, but he was used to this more than his brothers and his mom were. He thrived in this kind of environment. He didn't need to have things lined up all nice and neat.

Most of the time.

Today, he did.

Shelby lifted the phone and tapped the screen. "Rhett lied. He has the key. He will be going to the bank. Call me as soon as you get this message." She handed him back her phone. "That should get his attention," she said. "I feel like I'm setting my brother up to walk into the lion's den."

"You're doing the complete opposite." He tapped the screen. That was it. Now, they waited. "When he calls, let me do the talking."

"He'll hang up in a second. Maybe I should start things off and explain to him that you're not the enemy."

Rhett rubbed the back of his neck. "You're going to have to tell him in less than a minute that I'm listening. Because once he knows, if he's uncomfortable, he'll still end the call." And Rhett would have no way of tracking it. The app he'd put on her cell wasn't the most accurate to begin with compared to the ones the police used, but it did the trick for tracking a location, which was what he needed. Legally, his mother and brothers couldn't use it. However, he had to keep Chris chatting for a specific length of time. If he didn't, the entire thing was useless.

But not necessarily the conversation. That could be helpful, depending on what Chris said.

"Fine. You can talk first. However, I need you to follow my script. Can you do that?"

She nodded. "Tell me what to say."

"You need to use your own words so it sounds authentic. However, I'll give you the basics." He shifted in his seat. Siblings had a code. At least, he and his brothers did. They never had to discuss it. They never even made it up. They just understood each other innately. Their language came in a glance or a tone conveyed in a word. It didn't take much.

If she was as close to her brother as she claimed, she could hint to something without Rhett knowing, even though he was damn fucking good at his job.

That thoroughly pissed him off. Royally.

"Ask him to come to me sooner. Tell him—no, *beg* him—not to go to the bank. If he—"

The phone buzzed.

"Just convince him." Rhett hit the green button a little aggressively with his finger as the phone shifted on the table. He tapped the speaker button.

Shelby swallowed. "Chris?"

"Tell me what's going down at the bank," Chris said.

"Come to Rhett's house." Shelby stared at the phone. "It's the safest place for you and Jackie. He's not the enemy in this."

Chris laughed, but it wasn't the kind of laugh where something was funny. It had a sarcastic ring to it. "Next thing you're going to tell me, is that he's not sitting right next to you, listening to this conversation."

"No, she's not," Rhett said, needing to cut through the bullshit. He reached across the table and took Shelby's hand, giving it a good squeeze. "Your sister is scared and confused. I can't help either of you if I don't have answers, and I can't protect you if you do something stupid."

"I need that key," Chris said.

"That's out of my hands." Rhett wasn't above lying to Chris about many things, but this wasn't one of them. "Unfortunately, that became evidence, and I can't get it."

"Take me off speaker," Chris said.

Rhett jumped to his feet and did as the man asked.

Shelby covered her mouth and gasped.

"It's going to be okay," Rhett said. "Go inside. Let me do what I do best." He turned and took three paces. It was time to deal with this and get it all out in the open. At least, with Chris. "Okay. I'm out of earshot." He hated doing that to Shelby, but if that was what it took to get Chris talking, so be it.

"Who the fuck are you to my sister?"

Rhett jerked his head. That was not what he'd expected to be the first thing out of Chris's mouth. "An old friend."

"Funny. She never mentioned you to me."

"Right now, all I care about is making sure you, Jackie, and Shelby are safe. I can't do that if you're still running and, frankly, lying to me." Rhett rubbed his temple. "But let's be real. You brought this to my door for a reason."

"I don't want my sister anywhere near this. I've been trying to keep her out of it. That's why I ran."

"Why did you pick Lighthouse Cove?" Rhett didn't believe in coincidences. There had to be a connection. A reason that Chris and Jackie had skipped out on their hometown in Jacksonville and landed where Rhett lived. Right where someone from Shelby's past lived, who happened to be a private investigator and also had a cop for a mom.

"We got off the interstate, and that's where we landed. That's all."

"Bullshit," Rhett said. "Next thing you're going to tell me is that you didn't have someone call Shelby and tell her to go to Lighthouse Cove to collect your belongings."

"So what if I did?" Chris said.

"And what about the *anonymous tip* the cops got about the necklace and where to find it? That's so weirdly random that it makes no fucking sense at all."

"Do you have it?"

"Why is it so important?" Rhett asked.

"I need that key. I can't let what's in that safety deposit box end up in the wrong hands."

"Are you saying the cops are the wrong people?"

"I'm not saying anything other than Jackie and I have a plan, and it's the only one that's going to work. It's also not illegal," Chris said. "Well, not *that* illegal."

"What about the counterfeit money that we found in your wallet?"

"Planted."

Rhett inched closer to the water. He stared out at the river. While alligators were everywhere, it was rare that anyone saw one. Maybe a couple of miles up the river where there weren't any houses. But today, he spotted a pair swimming toward Trapper Joe's. Well, it *was* mating season.

"By whom, and why would they do that?"

"It's a long story, and we don't have time for this. I can't have what's in that safety deposit box made public. Not yet. It has to be done my way. So, if you or the cops have the key, I need your word that you will protect the contents."

"Come to my house now. If you explain what's in there and why it's important, I'm sure I can talk the police into keeping it private. I am the son of the chief."

"So I found out," Chris said. "But I can't afford to be arrested or brought in for questioning. Can you please tell me if you have the key?"

"I only want to help. That's the truth," Rhett said. "We have the key." His mother would have his fucking head on a platter and serve it to the alligators for lunch.

"I'll be at your place in an hour."

The phone went dead. Rhett lowered his cell from his ear and stared at it. The man he'd just spoken to wasn't someone strung out on drugs. He hadn't slurred his words, and his message had been loud and clear.

Rhett tapped on the app. He'd been on the phone long enough to get a location within about a three-mile radius but not precise coordinates.

It was close enough.

He zoomed in on the map. It appeared that Chris and Jackie were about forty minutes south of Lighthouse Cove. If Chris were smart—and Rhett was beginning to think Shelby's brother was smarter than he'd given the guy credit for—he'd be hitting the road now so he could sneak into the neighborhood.

Though that would be hard since it was gated with a guard at both sides.

He'd have to wait this one out. There was no point in trying to scramble to get someone to see if they could locate Chris now.

"Hey, Siri, call Emmerson."

It rang once.

"Hey, bro. What's up?"

"I spoke with Chris," Rhett said.

"Shelby's brother? That's big news."

Rhett glanced over his shoulder. Shelby stood on the other side of the sliding glass door. His heart tightened, but he was glad that she'd listened to his request and had gone inside. "He says he's going to be at my place in an hour."

"That changes things."

"It gets more interesting. He also told me that he needs whatever is in that safety deposit box, but he wants the contents protected. Something about it not going public."

"What does that mean?" Emmerson asked.

"I'm not exactly sure, but he's adamant that he hasn't done anything *too* illegal, and that someone—he didn't mention who—planted the counterfeit money."

"That's also interesting. Because, get this…" Emmerson said. "There were no prints on the bill. Not a single one. Totally clean."

"That's not possible."

"Exactly," Emmerson said.

"Chris told Jackie he had to run, which was why he left everything behind. That he barely had time to snag his keys. If we believe that scenario, the bad guys turned the place over, didn't find the key, and left the money behind so we'd think Chris was a criminal. And, he basically admitted that he was the one who tipped us off to the necklace."

"That actually makes sense."

"Well, now that I'm sitting here waiting for him to show up, I can't go with you to the bank." Of course, his mother wasn't on board with that anyway. "However, I need you to run some interference and let Mom in on some of this, especially who might be lurking in the background. AKA, the mob."

"Absolutely. I'll make sure we have more officers on hand. I'll tell Mom to handle whatever is inside carefully and call you as soon as I know anything."

"You'll be with her, right? Or Emmett?"

"I'll be there," Emmerson said. "Talk to you later."

Rhett ended the call and tucked his cell into his back pocket. He turned on his heels, took two steps, and paused.

Shelby came flying out the door. "What happened?" She charged him like a wild boar.

He resisted the urge to back up. He grounded himself and prepared to be toppled. "Chris and Jackie are on their way here."

"Seriously?"

"That's what he said." Rhett's blood raced through his system as he stared into her intense orbs. It was as if he could see right into her soul. He grabbed her by the hips and steadied them both. "Emmerson will take point on whatever's happening at the bank. You and I will sit tight here. Everything's going to be fine."

Tears flowed down her cheeks. "Are you sure?"

He couldn't be completely honest about that. A million and one things could go wrong, and he had no idea what was in store for his family at the bank, especially when it came to the bad guys. But he had to trust the process. This wasn't the first time the Kirbys had been caught in the crossfire.

And it wouldn't be the last.

"Yes. It's all going to be fine."

"I wish I could believe that."

He brushed some of her hair over her shoulder before cupping the back of her neck. Memories of waking up with her in his arms in Key West collided with thoughts of last night. Those mornings had been the sweetest moments of his life. He'd never forgotten them. As a matter of fact, he'd cherished them, locking them away in a special place inside his brain. He let them out on special occasions when he either needed a pick-me-up or wanted to torture himself.

It sounded strange, but thoughts of those three weeks served two different purposes in his life. They tormented his heart while they also reminded him that he was a man who loved deeply.

But he'd put his heart under lock and key, never to be allowed near a woman again.

Only now, staring at Shelby, his heart demanded release and begged to be given to her on a silver platter. It ached to love her, and it didn't care if she loved him back. It was willing to take the risk.

Especially after last night. He'd become the kind of man who accepted that he might never have her forever, so he'd take her right here and now.

Even if Rhett's mind kept yelling at him not to kiss her. Not to allow her back into his heart.

It was too late.

He took her mouth, hot and hard. He couldn't resist, and he couldn't stop. Not unless she made him, and then he'd stand down.

But she pulled him closer, wrapping her arms tightly around his body.

Her tongue greeted his with power and passion. She took over the kiss, deepening it. His muscles twitched, and fire filled his belly. His insides came alive as if they'd been asleep for the last five years.

He lifted her into his arms and carried her across the patio.

"We shouldn't do this again," she whispered.

"Okay." Carefully, and without dropping her on her ass, he opened the slider and stepped into the kitchen. "For the record, I want it noted that you're the one who wants to stop."

"Didn't say that I did. Just mentioned it wasn't the smartest thing we've ever done because—put me down for a second."

Well, that really killed the mood. But he had to admit; it was for the best. Using sex right now to pass the time and avoid certain fears and emotions wasn't the right thing. He set her on her feet.

She tucked her hair behind her ears. "I have to be honest."

"I'm listening."

"I loved being with you last night."

"I'm not complaining." He leaned against the counter, wishing it wasn't too early for a cocktail.

Not only that, but he was technically working, and he preferred to keep a clear head about him while on the job. "I want you to know that I wasn't using you, if that's where this conversation is going."

"I didn't—don't—feel used, but maybe you should."

He laughed. "I don't. You're hurting. You're scared. We have a history."

"We didn't five years ago."

She had a point, but he chose to ignore that statement. For now. "Perhaps. But let's not overanalyze last night."

"All right." She climbed up onto the stool and let out a sigh. "Although—and don't let this go to your head—you're a really great kisser."

He brushed his fingers across her shoulder and smiled. "Too late. You just inflated my ego. And if you pop it, I might have to go swim with the alligators."

She flashed her pearly whites and laughed.

It was music to his ears. He'd always loved the way she laughed. It tickled his senses like the soft breeze coming in from the river. For the three weeks he'd known her five years ago, she'd had a heavy heart.

Today was no different.

He wanted to change that for her any way he could.

Even if that meant he let her use his body to soothe her soul. He didn't care what it did to him, as long as she got some peace.

"I'm here for you. One hundred percent. Whatever you need—and I mean that." He slipped up onto the stool next to hers and took her hand. "I still care about you." There was a strong part of him that wanted to fight all the feelings currently taking over his mind and heart. He'd done it five years ago; he could do it again.

It would be hard, but he was a strong man, both physically and emotionally. He'd battle through if he had to.

But he was tired of doing it. He worked through his broken heart with Krista and found Shelby, only to have to protect it from being crushed once again.

But did he really have to do that?

Or had he wasted the last five years of his life?

"I care about you, too," she said softly.

"Can I ask you a question?"

"You just did," she said.

He chuckled. He'd missed her sarcasm and quick wit. "What do you think might have happened if I had called you five years ago? Where do you think it would have gone?"

"Didn't we kind of go over this?"

"No. We danced around it in a very polite fashion. Now that I know we're both still insanely attracted to each other I want to know the deeper answer." He hoped he didn't come off as a desperate man. He could survive if she opted to keep things on the surface. His life would go on if she brushed all of this under the rug.

It would be nice if they could get all their real emotions on the table.

"I don't know," she said. "I was hyper-focused on my brother. Maybe too much. And if you're asking me to be honest, I might have been using that to get over you not calling, which probably wasn't all that healthy."

Rhett pounded his chest. "That hurt."

"You asked me to tell you the truth."

He nodded.

"Back then, I wished I had you to lean on. But then again, I never told you about Chris or the situation, so I think every time my phone rang, I was afraid that it *was* you and wondered what I should tell you."

"Did you think I might feel differently about you because of your brother?"

"I questioned whether you felt anything for me at all since you never bothered to pick up the phone."

"I guess I deserve that." He cupped her chin. "I felt—I *feel*—a lot for you. Five years ago, I didn't think I could give you the whole me or enough of me to even try at any kind of relationship. And, as it turned out, you weren't capable either, considering you couldn't even tell me you had a brother."

"It wasn't like that," she said. "It wasn't for me to tell anyone his problems."

"I'm not talking about his struggles. I'm talking about his existence. I told you about all my brothers, but I didn't mention anything about what any of them might be going through. Just that I had them." He dropped his hand to his lap. He didn't mean to sound angry or resentful, though his tone certainly rang harshly. "I'm sorry. I didn't mean for this to turn into anything but wondering what might have been if I'd been a stronger man at the time. I'm not upset that you were protecting your brother. However, I'd be lying if I said that I'm not a little hurt that you didn't trust me with the knowledge that you had one."

"Now you know."

"I do," Rhett said. "I'm looking forward to meeting him and his girlfriend. More importantly, I want to help them put whatever this bullshit is behind them. And us, too." He rested his hand on her shoulder. "Since having sex a second time as a distraction is off the table, want to play a game of backgammon? I bet I can still kick your ass."

She tossed her head back and laughed. "Bring it."

He leaned over and kissed her cheek. He wanted more, but this would be good enough for now. After her brother got here and they straightened everything out, he'd pursue her the right way.

8

Shelby glanced at her watch while she waited for Rhett to make his move. Why he contemplated it for so long was beyond her. The game wasn't that hard, and no matter his choice—thanks to the roll of the dice—he would leave himself wide-open for her to push one of his pieces off the board.

"What time did Chris say he was going to be here?" Her heart had been pounding in her throat for the last twenty minutes. The anticipation of seeing her brother was unbearable. She didn't know if she would hug him. Or slap him.

Or both.

Rhett ran a hand across his cheeks and down his chin. That wasn't a good sign. The few times he'd done that before, it was because he wasn't thrilled about the situation. "He should have been here by now."

"Then why are we sitting here playing a stupid game?"

He reached out and took her hand. "A friend of mine is checking the area where I pinged your brother's phone. There are only two hotels, and I should be hearing any minute." He picked up his cell from the coffee table and waved it. "My brother Miles sometimes does work for me on the side—"

"The mechanic?"

"Yeah. But he's also a licensed private investigator. Pisses off my mother that he'd do that for me and not become a cop. Anyway, he's been checking things out at the front gate and around the neighborhood. He hasn't seen anything or your brother. Yet."

"You really think Chris would sneak around before driving down the street?" Shelby had spent the last six weeks of her life preoccupied with the thought that her brother had been using drugs again. It was so bad that she'd started driving by Chris's old stomping grounds. Not once did she ever see her brother there, even when she thought for sure that was where he would be, especially when he lied about his location. The realization that she knew very little about her brother hit her gut like a sledgehammer.

"I would if I were him. He has no idea what he's walking into. Or if he can trust me."

She jumped to her feet. "I'm his sister. I'm the most trustworthy person in his life."

"I'm sure you are." He stood slowly and took her by the forearms, lowering his chin. "I don't pretend to know what's going on with Chris and Jackie. But I suspect all he's been trying to do is protect you from whatever he's running from. If I had a sister, I wouldn't want her involved in anything like this, and I can tell you that all my brothers would want to keep their wives from any kind of harm, too. You must believe that he's had your best interests in mind from the very beginning."

She wished she could honestly believe that, but there were so many things she didn't know and didn't understand. It was hard to wrap her brain around any of it. Her eyes felt like sandpaper. She had no tears left for her brother. Only anger and frustration filled her gut. "I feel like he's manipulating all of us."

"He kind of is," Rhett said. "But don't be mad at him for that. Not until we know all the facts."

"Honestly, it's hard not to be pissed as hell at him," she admitted. She leaned into Rhett's strong frame, wrapping her arms around his waist. "The more I think about how he disappeared, how he came here, and how he seems to be orchestrating all of this, I want to strangle him."

"I can understand that, but until we have answers, you're only going to make yourself crazy thinking about all the unknowns. We need to wait this—"

"But for how long?" She grabbed Rhett's cell from his back pocket, where he always carried it. She stared at a screen that told her she'd failed facial recognition and needed a passcode. "I'm going nuts here. I need to do something, and the fact that you're doing jack shit is pissing me off."

He quickly snatched his phone from her fingers and turned his back. He pressed it to his ear and completely ignored her.

How rude.

She planted her hands on her hips and tapped her toe.

"Hey. It's me," he said. "Can you give me an update?"

Her heart beat so fast she could feel it in her muscles. They twitched and pulsed. It hurt, and she just wanted all of this to end. Now. She resented her brother for putting her through this, and she mentally chided herself for allowing it to be all-consuming.

About a minute ticked by, and she wished she could hear the other side of the conversation.

"Well, Chris hasn't shown. Miles has been lurking, but there's been no action. Nothing. I will text my buddy who is checking out the two hotels around where I pinged Chris's cell and do a complete sweep here, but he should have been here twenty minutes ago. I checked traffic. There wasn't any. Of course, he could have taken the scenic route, but I doubt it. He wants what's in that box."

Rhett took a step toward the kitchen and scratched the back of his head. "Yeah. I thought of that. Do you want me to come?" Rhett turned and caught her gaze. "That's true."

She narrowed her stare. A million questions with no answers swirled in her brain.

"All right. Thanks." Rhett tapped the screen. "Okay. Emmerson and Emmett are at the bank. They are keeping an eye out for your brother and Jackie."

She let out a gasp. "It makes sense they would go there."

"It does," Rhett admitted. "Come on. We need to go for a ride around the block and then head to the police station."

"What? Why?"

"Because whatever is in that safety deposit box has to be logged into evidence. I'm sorry. But that's the way it's got to be." He raised his hand. "My brothers and mom have promised that it will be kept confidential unless it's mind-blowing and completely criminal. But we need to get your brother to come in. So, can I please have your phone." He phrased it as a command, not a question.

She knew she had to give her cell to Rhett. This was real life-and-death shit. She pointed toward the coffee table.

He leaned over and picked it up.

"You know the passcode," she said. Her eyes burned, but there were no tears.

"Hey." He pulled her into his arms and crushed her against his chest. "I know you're scared and want your brother to be here and safe. I do, too. I really do. I'm going to call him and see what's going on." He brushed his warm lips across the side of her cheek. They inched closer to her mouth, kissing tenderly.

It was impossible to resist the comfort he offered, and the hardest part was that she knew it was real. Nothing about the emotions that swirled between the two of them was fake, and she wanted to explore them. Only she couldn't.

He cupped her face, breaking off the kiss. "Let me call your brother."

"Okay."

While he was busy with her cell, she decided to put the board game away. Doing something tactile made her feel useful. Keeping her mind and body occupied was better than sitting idle and feeling as though she had no control over anything.

Her entire life had been like that, and she was tired of it. She wanted that to change. She wanted to take charge but had never really known how.

Five years ago, when she spent those three glorious weeks with Rhett in Key West, she'd had a taste of what that could feel like, and she wanted more. But her brain was wired to make sure her brother and father were taken care of before she met her needs.

"Right to voicemail," Rhett said with a huge dose of frustration. "I'll text him and try again, but

I don't like that, and I can't ping the location with my tracker." Rhett stared at her cell. "Shit. The text isn't being delivered."

"What does that mean?"

"Either the phone is off, or it's dead."

"That doesn't sound good." Next time she saw him, she was going to wring her brother's neck, not hug him for putting her through this bullshit.

"Come on. I want to leave a message for him at the gate. If and when he shows up, Miles will be here."

She reached out and grabbed Rhett's arm. "I don't know how to thank you for all this. Or your family. I know I've been all over the map and acting like a crazy woman, but—"

He pressed his finger to her lips. "There's nothing abnormal about how you're behaving, and I want to be the person who's here for you."

Her heart dropped to her toes and lurched to the back of her throat as his mouth took hers in a passionate kiss. It felt as if her entire body lifted right off the ground for a moment. It was quick, but it packed a ton of emotion that she didn't know where to file.

"Why do you always do that?" she asked.

"Do what?"

She glared, pressing her fingers to her lips.

"I can't help myself. Your mouth is a magnet for my lips." He took her by the hand and tugged her toward the garage. "Let's go."

Her lips tingled, sending shockwaves through the rest of her system.

That kiss would get her through the rest of whatever the day brought.

Rhett tried Chris four times on the ride to the police station, and it went straight to voicemail each time. That concerned him for two different reasons.

The first one could be because Chris had played Rhett—which he'd considered the second he'd agreed to have Chris come to the house. It had been something in the back of his mind immediately.

However, Rhett didn't believe that Chris had stood him up. Not in that moment. And not now. Something else had happened. Either Chris got spooked or…something worse.

He pulled into his brother Nathan's parking spot. It annoyed some of the other officers, but it was a perk of being the chief of police's son. If one of his brothers or even his mom were off duty, and he knew, he could use the spot if—and only if—he was there on police business.

Or to visit family, which was kind of the same thing.

He turned his Jeep off and took Shelby's hand. "Are you okay? You haven't said a word the entire ride."

She shifted in her seat and stared at him with an intense glare. Her eyes were wide with thick emotion.

Things he hadn't seen before rose to the surface. She'd been broken when he first met her, and he knew it. It was something that'd bonded them in a weird way, but it was also the thing that had driven them apart. He couldn't give himself until he fixed the things inside him that had his gut and heart twisted.

What he failed to understand then was that he'd been his own worst enemy, and all he needed was to let go of the toxicity and open his mind to reality.

But when reality walked in, he was blind to her, and she wasn't ready to let go of the pains of the past.

"I've spent my entire life taking care of everyone in my family. I did it because I thought that was what family did. I thought that was what loyalty and love were all about."

He squeezed her hand and smiled. "It is," he said. "However, and please don't take this the wrong way, you had to grow up too quickly. You were forced to take on a mothering role when you should have been playing dress-up with your friends. You never got a chance to be a kid, so you really take it to heart when your only living relative hurts. Or worse, disappears." Rhett wanted her to understand that this wasn't a typical situation. And that while what she was feeling wasn't abnormal, perhaps her responses to her brother over the years had been overprotective and a bit overbearing.

Much like how Rhett had closed himself off to protecting his heart from being hurt. It was a defense mechanism, and all it did was hurt him in the long run. Where he thought he was living life in a way that gave him freedom, all he was doing was living in a cage.

She'd been doing the same thing. She wanted to take care of her family. If her brother was okay, *she* was okay. He suspected that, in her mind, she felt she could journey out and find her life when that happened. Seek her inner happiness. But that was never the case because during those few years when it had been smooth-sailing with Chris, she was sitting around waiting for the other shoe to drop.

"I'm angry that he didn't come to me. I thought we were close."

"That's why he didn't come to you," Rhett said. "Look. I've got six brothers, and we're as thick as thieves. We all have different relationships with one another. Seth and Nathan are two peas in a pod. Emmett and Emmerson are like the same person sometimes. And Jamison and Emmerson are tight. They did everything together growing up, which was weird. Miles and I are cut from the same cloth. But if I want advice about something, I go to either Emmett or Jamison. They get me in ways that my other brothers don't. However, when I was going through my struggles with Krista really bad, I didn't go to any of them. Not even Emmett, though he knew and sent me to Key West. And when I came home, I didn't talk about you to anyone. Emmett had to practically beat it out of me."

"I'm not really sure how to take that statement."

He ran his thumb across her cheek. He hated seeing any kind of pain or anger etched in her expression. It didn't matter that he hadn't put it there, it still physically cut him to the bone. "My point is that sometimes I didn't want to burden my brothers, especially when they were sick and tired of something they wanted me to be over. They were tired of Krista and her bullshit. They hated how she treated me and didn't understand my obsession with her."

"I think this is different."

"I know it is incredibly different, and perhaps my example is minimizing the situation," Rhett said. "But you've been taking care of your little brother for as long as he can remember. He doesn't want you to do that anymore. He wants to take care of himself, and he wants to protect you. And it's time for you to realize you've never really taken care of yourself. You've never had your own life because you've refused to detach yourself from everyone else."

She opened her mouth, but he hushed her with his finger. "That doesn't mean you should stop loving them or being there for them. But it does mean you have to let him be his own man. Even if he were to slip and start using again. He's…what? Two years younger than you, so, thirty-three?"

She nodded. "He was twenty-eight when treatment finally took. He started using when he was a teenager. Hard drugs before he was fifteen. He barely had a chance. Before I dropped him off, he nearly died. He'd been in the hospital after an accidental overdose. I thought I'd lost him." She blinked out a tear. "I'm worried I won't ever see him again now."

"What I want you to hold onto is the fact that he's playing this as smart as he can. I generally don't take too kindly to being used the way he has, but he led you to Lighthouse Cove because he knew about me. And about my family. He tipped off the local police department about the necklace and key." He pointed toward the building. "Not the county sheriff's office or the state police, but my mother's office. Your little brother might have gotten himself into some trouble, but he's all grown up and making the same kinds of choices I would if I ever found myself in his situation. And, trust me, I've been in some sticky places."

"That really doesn't make me feel better."

Out of the corner of his eye, Rhett saw his brother Emmerson peek his head out the front door and wave.

"We'd better go inside." He leaned in and kissed her cheek. "We're going to find him. I promise." He knew that he might not be able to keep his word, but he would die trying. Jumping out of the driver's side of his Jeep, he raced around the hood of the

SUV and pulled open the door for Shelby. He placed his hand on the small of her back and guided her to the door. "Relax," he whispered in her ear.

"Easy for you to say. That's your family in there. I feel like I'm walking into the lion's den."

He chuckled. "When I was a kid, my mom would sometimes summon me to the station after school. I always thought I was in trouble, but then I'd get here, and she'd have a bag of cookies and milk and we'd sit and chat in her office."

"That's kind of cute."

"It was her way of making up for her long, crazy hours." He pulled open the door. "But also, she was trying to scare me shitless because there was always some goon sitting in the waiting room. I learned later that he was a private investigator or someone she knew and not a criminal. She just wanted me to think that."

"That's funny, especially since you became a P.I."

"Yeah. She regrets that part." Rhett waved to the officer at the desk, who buzzed him past the lobby. He strolled down the hallway toward the conference room, where he'd been told to go.

"Who all is going to be here?"

"To my knowledge, just Emmerson. My mom has some meeting, and Emmett is out on patrol." He wrapped his arm tighter around her waist, letting his hand rest on her curvy hip. The more time he spent with her, the more he was reminded why the memory of her came to him in his dreams.

And his daily thoughts.

It wasn't the same kind of obsession he had experienced with Krista. That had been based on an unhealthy relationship that had been two-sided in the sense that Krista continued to be in his face, dangling the carrot, even when she'd been involved with someone else.

And he followed her around like a sick puppy.

She'd been the first woman he'd ever loved, and he'd let her control him in ways he still didn't understand.

Things hadn't been that way with Shelby.

While neither of them had been honest, things *were* easy. Natural. And real.

He wanted to find a way to ask her if they could spend some time getting to know each other without the stress of other people. Date. He didn't care if he had to drive to Jacksonville to do it. He wanted the opportunity to find out if what he felt could withstand the test of time.

The fact of the matter was that she was eight years younger than him. Not that he was old, but it seemed like she had more time to settle down and figure things out.

Whereas this felt as if it were his last chance at love. At a family.

He stumbled over that thought. It was dramatic and unexpected. He had no idea his mind was going in that direction.

"This way." He waved his hand in front of the conference room.

"Come on in," Emmerson said. "Have a seat."

"Did anyone see or hear from my brother?" Shelby asked.

Emmerson shook his head. "I wish we had. We did however have some other visitors."

"Who, exactly?" Rhett asked as he pulled out a chair for Shelby.

She eased into her seat.

Rhett stood behind her with his hands on her shoulders, rubbing gently. He half-expected her to push him away, but, thankfully, she didn't.

"Emmett is working that exact part of the equation, but there were two men in a dark sedan in the parking lot. They saw us and split."

"How did they know what bank if they didn't have the key?"

"That's where Chris might have made his first big mistake," Emmerson said. "It's a Florida SunTrust, so they have branches as far north as Jacksonville, and both he and Jackie have personal accounts there. We only have one branch in a fifty-mile radius, and since they knew Chris had been in the area, it made sense."

"Okay. So how did they know Chris was here?" That question had been bothering Rhett for days.

"Another mistake that Chris couldn't have known about. We found a tracking app on Jackie's phone. So, whoever the bad guy is, they followed them right to Lighthouse Cove." Emmerson pushed a stack of papers across the table. "And it appears the bad guy is her uncle."

"What's this?" Rhett reached across Shelby and snagged the paperwork.

"The contents of the safety deposit box. I'm not exactly sure why they don't want this to go public unless they are protecting her uncle—which doesn't make sense. You'll see when you read it," Emmerson said. "But to paraphrase, when Jackie was six, her parents were murdered, and it went unsolved. Only, it didn't." Emmerson tapped his knuckles on the table. "That right there is proof that Joe Staub murdered his own brother and sister-in-law."

"Are you serious?" Shelby asked. "Why? That makes no sense." She turned and stared at Rhett. "Is he joking or something?"

"No. This is real." Rhett continued thumbing through the file that was filled with images, police reports, and other shit that'd somehow been suppressed and tossed out the window like it didn't matter.

Someone had paid a lot of money to ensure that this never saw the light of day, and someone else took the fall.

Well, not literally, since no one ended up in jail.

"We don't have all the connections yet," Emmerson said. "But I have to wonder if this is why Joe Staub came running to Florida."

"Sounds more like he was banished to the south," Rhett said.

"And when he came here, he made a connection to the Mortellis by taking out a *business* loan. But what's weird about that, is it's the only thing her uncle ever did with the Mortellis that is questionable."

"That is odd," Rhett said. "I know some people

who can ask around inside the Gorga organization to see if Joe is on any shit lists of any kind, or if they are looking for proof. Although, I can understand why Joe Staub wants this hidden."

"My head is spinning," Shelby said softly. "I looked into this when Jackie and Chris started dating. Sort of."

"On the surface, there are only rumors about the Staub brothers and their connection to the Gorgas. Jackie's parents' murder was the biggest one, but nothing was ever proven," Emmerson said.

"Based on what is in this file,"—Rhett turned a page—"there has been one hell of a cover-up."

"I know," Emmerson said.

"The Gorga family denied any connection, so the police looked elsewhere. According to what I found, there was some buzz at the time about the Gorgas and the Staubs, but it died down, and now it's a cold case."

"If that police report comes out, which it has to, a bunch of people will have a lot to say." Emmerson sat on the edge of the table. "We can't suppress this for very long."

"Why not?" Shelby pushed her chair back and reached for the papers, but Rhett jerked them back.

He knew that if his mother were in the station,

Shelby would be sitting in the waiting room. She wouldn't want this discussed in front of a family member. Rhett owed his brother one for allowing Shelby to be part of the process. He knew his brother was putting himself on the line, and he appreciated the gesture. But he also knew that showing Shelby the documents wasn't a good idea. While Rhett wasn't done going through them, he handed them back to Emmerson. If Emmerson wanted Rhett to know something, he would get Rhett that information one way or another.

"Someone committed murder, and then a cover-up happened. It needs to be investigated. This all needs to go up to New Jersey," Emmerson said. "Mom hasn't seen these, and she's letting me be the lead on this. She's tied up for a few more hours, and I'll be able to get her to give us probably until end of day tomorrow to find Chris and Jackie. Even she'll see the urgency of hearing their side, and she'll want the opportunity to review everything before bringing in other agencies and possibly jumping the gun on something we don't fully understand."

Shelby stood, smoothing down the front of her jeans. Her jaw was tight, and stress lined her forehead.

Rhett puffed out his chest, impressed by how she kept her composure, even though he could feel the anger and frustration filling the air around him.

"Why would Jackie and my brother want this hidden? I would think they would want to expose this, especially if her uncle's the one chasing them."

"I've got a couple of theories on that," Emmerson said. "One of them is ass-backward."

Rhett knew where his brother was going because his mind had started to backtrack there, as well. "Are you suggesting that perhaps the Gorgas asked Joe to kill his brother, and this came from them? That they have been controlling him from New Jersey with this and giving him his freedom but having him do little favors so this will stay hidden?"

"That's one theory. We haven't been able to put eyes on Joe, which makes me think that these papers would put him in hot water with the Gorgas if it came out. So, he has to protect them. But it could work the other way, as well." Emmerson leaned against the back counter.

"Meaning he can't afford for the information to come out, or the Gorgas will send someone to kill him." Rhett rolled his neck. No matter how this played out, they were dealing with some bad people.

"Exactly," Emmerson said.

"Do we know where Tony Gorga and his goons are?" Rhett asked, taking Shelby's hand. It was a lot for him to take in, so he suspected it was even more for her. His phone buzzed. But it wasn't a call. It was one of his outside motion detectors. Specifically, the one on his dock. He stole a quick glance. Shit. He needed to open the app.

What struck him as odd was that Miles had texted about ten minutes ago, stating that he'd done a second sweep of the area and had found nothing.

Rhett had told him to hang tight down the street, where he felt there was one weak spot by the golf course. There wasn't a lot of traffic since it was a dead-end, and anyone could jump the fence. It had been a bone of contention when he bought the house. He'd brought it up with the homeowners' association and the guardhouse. They'd agreed that it was something they needed to address.

Of course, anyone could access the neighborhood by water.

Which was why he'd added cameras and motion detectors at the dock.

"Tony is in New Jersey, along with most of the

big players. They don't have ties to Mortelli. But if Hector Mortelli thinks Joe Staub has ever done anything to cross another mob family and knows there's proof… That's not going to be pretty for Joe. Regardless, this isn't good for Jackie's uncle."

Shelby held up both hands. "What I don't understand is why my brother would hide this stuff. What do he and Jackie have to gain? All they had to do was give it to the police. I don't understand why they wanted to keep it from you. Or why they want it kept out of the press. It doesn't make—" She closed her eyes and let out a long breath before blinking them open. "Someone is threatening them, and they think holding onto that is their ticket to safety."

"That's a good bet. The questions are: Who, and why? It seems obvious that Joe wouldn't want this to be in the cops' hands. And maybe he's keeping it from Tony Gorga." Rhett waited for his app to run live. Sometimes, technology drove him batshit crazy. He texted Miles to return to his house but warned him not to spook whoever was there. He wanted Chris and Jackie to feel as though they had been successful in breaching his security.

"One thing really bothers me about this." Emmerson held up a document that he'd pulled from the files. "This is the autopsy report for Joe's brother. Jackie's father. There is a page missing. The one that gives the cause of death."

"That's odd," Rhett said. "But the medical examiner's office should have another copy."

"One would think so," Emmerson said. "However, I haven't requested it yet. If this cover-up goes deep—and I suspect it does—and someone was paid off to let Joe Staub go free, there's a crooked medical examiner, or both…" Emmerson arched a brow. "I'm not ready to tip off anyone in New Jersey that we're poking around this case yet."

"That could be smart, but what's the payoff?" Rhett scrolled through the app. A few blurred images of two people pulling kayaks onto his dock appeared.

"That's the million-dollar question," Emmerson said. "If Tony Gorga knew about this,"— Emmerson tapped the papers—"then I have to believe he pitted brother against brother and made a promise he never intended to keep. And that he has the last piece of the puzzle."

"That's weak," Rhett said. "My money's on the idea that Joe used every penny he had to pay off the ME and then hauled ass to Florida. I think we take a chance and reach out to the medical examiner."

"We can't. He died in a car crash a month after this report," Emmerson said. "Drove right into a tree. His brakes failed."

"That's fucking suspicious," Rhett said.

"Agreed, and why I don't want to call anyone in that office until I have a better understanding and a few more details." Emmerson nodded. "Look. I've got a lot of shit to do with this case before Mom gets back."

"We'll get out of your way." Rhett took Shelby by the hand and led her out of the conference room, down the hall, through the lobby, and outside.

"What's the rush?" she asked when he opened the Jeep door.

"I think your brother is at my house." He practically pushed her into the vehicle. "I want to get there before someone else sees him. I want to find out what's really going on so we can devise a plan before I bring my brother in on this. Because once I do that, some things are out of my hands." He hoped Chris stayed right where he was for the next fifteen minutes. Or there would be hell to pay.

9

*S*helby jumped out of the Jeep as soon as it rolled to a stop in Rhett's driveway.

"Wait," Rhett called.

No way would she do anything of the sort, not when her brother was somewhere on the property. She pulled on the front door, but it was locked. She raced toward the side of the house, but a strong arm wrapped around her middle. "Let me go!"

"He's not here," Rhett whispered softly in her ear. "He was. But he's gone."

"What?" She spun on her heels. "How do you know?"

"By the time Miles got here, Chris and Jackie were gone."

"Why aren't we following them?"

"Miles tried. He got on my boat, thinking that because Chris and Jackie were in a couple of kayaks, it would be easy, but it was low tide, and they went upriver where it was too shallow. We can take my smaller boat in about an hour as the river rises. But I suspect, they had a car at the park and are long gone by now."

"Why? Why did they even bother coming here then?" She stared at him with tears burning in her eyes and anger tearing through her heart. Nothing made sense.

"For this," a strange voice said from somewhere behind her.

"Shelby, this is my brother, Miles." Rhett held her close to his body.

She wanted to resent how much she needed that support, but if he didn't hold her up, she feared that she might crumble.

"It's nice to finally meet you." Miles, who looked a lot like Rhett except with much shorter hair and a few extra inches of height, stood in front of her with a kind smile. "I'm sorry for the circumstances, though."

She swallowed. "Did you see or talk with Chris and Jackie?"

"By the time I got here, they were kayaking at a

good clip down the river I couldn't catch them because of how low the tide is," Miles said. "But they left a note."

"Let's go inside." Rhett led her back toward the front of the house.

Her legs felt as if she'd been swimming for hours. They barely held her upright. She squared her shoulders, tired of feeling as though she wasn't in control of her life. "But you saw them. And they looked okay?"

"I took a picture." Miles paused at the front stoop and held up his cell. "And Rhett's cameras can be played back. Your brother is alive and well."

"Thank you for that."

Rhett unlocked the door.

"Can I have the note?" Shelby asked as she stepped into the hallway, heading toward the kitchen.

"It was actually addressed to Rhett," Miles said.

"Give it to her." Rhett squeezed her arm. "Would you like something to drink?"

"A shot of tequila would be nice." She took the note with shaky fingers. She wanted to run into her room and lock the door, but she knew that wouldn't go over well, so she pulled up a stool and stared at the envelope with Rhett's name written in her brother's handwriting.

She'd recognize it anywhere. Her brother had the neatest penmanship of anyone she knew, and she always teased him that it looked like a girl's. He just laughed and told her she was jealous.

Which was a true statement, but not in a negative way.

"Listen, I have a friend who works at the park," Miles said. "I'm going to race up there now because Annie hasn't seen anyone that looks like your brother and Jackie leave today."

"That's interesting," Rhett said. "Could those kayaks have been rentals?"

"The park ones don't have any identifying marks. So, yeah, they could have been."

"Maybe we should go with you." With trembling fingers, Shelby flipped open the edges of the envelope.

"No. Let my brother handle this. We don't want to spook Chris any more than he already is. The park is only a few miles up the road."

"Besides, he doesn't know me or what I drive. He'll see the two of you coming a mile away and probably run. Me? I can move around a little more freely. Plus, the bad guys might be looking for you, Shelby."

"Keep me posted." Rhett gave his brother a man hug before setting a glass of tequila on the rocks in front of Shelby.

She lifted it to her lips and sipped. It went down as smooth as butter. She tugged the paper out of the envelope and unfolded it. "Did your brother read this?"

"No," Rhett said.

"Why not?"

"Because he was too busy trying to chase them down, and then I was five minutes out and asked him to wait," Rhett said.

She lifted her gaze and caught Rhett's. He stared back at her with the most loving eyes she'd ever seen. They were deep blue pools of kindness. She could dive into them and swim around forever, never drowning. She took his hand and shifted her attention back to the note, reading aloud as she read to herself.

Rhett.

First. Thank you for taking care of my sister. I had to bring her here for her own safety. I didn't know what else to do. I had no intention of you getting that key. Or the information. Unfor-

tunately, I was found before my sister arrived, and you found my hotel room. Nothing is as it seems when it comes to all of this, and Jackie's father isn't dead. Albert Staub lives. We must protect him. We can't afford for any of this to come out. I'm not ready to come in or tell you the whole story. Just please, keep my sister safe. They will come after her because of me and Jackie. But even though they followed me here, they won't know to look for you. I took care of that. When it's safe, I'll be in touch.

Chris.

Shelby tilted her head. "Again, how does he even know about you? I never talked to him about you. I even asked him, but he didn't tell me. I don't understand. I need to understand."

Rhett took the note from her hands and took a picture of it with his cell before tapping away on the screen. "Did you keep a diary or a journal?"

"Yes."

"Did you write about me? Could he have learned about me that way?" His focus remained everywhere but on her, and that boiled her blood. She flicked her fingers on his biceps.

"Ouch." He jerked. "What the hell was that for?"

"Doesn't it concern you how my brother knew to connect you to all of this?"

Rhett raised the note. "What concerns me more

is the fact that Albert Staub is alive and the questions that raises. Like was Joe the one who was murdered? Did Jackie know any of this? She was just a baby when it happened, but would she know the difference between her uncle and her dad if it was really her uncle who was murdered? Or was that body someone else? And how much more of this was covered up and why? And then there is how it affects Jackie's and your brother's safety. So, I'm sending all this to Miles and contemplating how much I want to tell Emmerson. He needs the information, but I think I might hold off until we know if Chris and Jackie are hiding out at the state park and whether Albert is with them—or if they know where he is."

She gasped. That was more important than the fact that her brother had gone through her things. Her journals. Her private diaries. The ones she didn't think he would dare read. The ones she'd left out in her office, right on her desk where her brother could sneak in and read them.

Which he obviously had. He'd been snooping around, and that was why she'd thought he was using again. He kept coming back into her house to read more about Rhett. To understand who he was and learn about his job, which she'd also written about in her journals. How fascinating she thought it was.

"Okay. But my diaries mention you and the fact that you live here. If the bad guys got those, they—"

"If he left them behind, I'm sure he hid them."

"They must have found them, because the bad guys are here," she said with a squeaky voice. She hated it when she sounded like a scared rat.

"Not necessarily. There was a tracker on Jackie's phone," Rhett said. "When was the last time you saw your diaries?"

"I don't know. I haven't written in them in a while."

"Perhaps Chris hid them. Or took them when he disappeared. I'll send someone to your house to check on things. Okay?"

She nodded. Her mind wandered to Trapper Joe's and the state park. She and her brother had gone there a couple of times when they were kids. Their mom hadn't enjoyed it, and they'd packed up and gone home early.

Shelby had returned for a trip in high school, though. She loved it and had vowed to go back someday.

Unfortunately, she never did, and she couldn't

imagine her brother *ever* going camping. At least, not when he'd been using. It wasn't the kind of thing he was into. But sober Chris was very different.

"It seems to me that camping there wouldn't be smart. It wouldn't be easy to escape. There's only one way out," she said.

"That's where you're wrong. They could take off by boat at high tide. Kayaks anytime. Hiking trails. Biking trails. If they have a camper with a car, they could leave the camper behind and just take the car. They could have more than one campsite. They could even be at one of the more remote sites by Trapper Joe's. Maybe Albert is there with him or is hiding somewhere else."

"Why are we sitting here on our asses, then? Let's go get my brother. We can bring him back here." She jumped to her feet and turned. "Don't you think he'd be safer with you?"

Rhett grabbed her wrist. "We're not going anywhere."

"Why not?"

"Because your brother made it clear that he doesn't want us to. And for now, I'm sort of going to respect that."

"What the hell does that mean?" Her heart beat

against her rib cage so hard, she thought it might crack one of her ribs. "He's running from some unknown mobster, and you're going to let him be a sitting duck?"

"He orchestrated an elaborate plan to bring you to me," Rhett said. "So far, the only thing that hasn't gone exactly the way he wanted is the contents of the safety deposit box. He's drawing someone out for a specific reason. Maybe he wants some kind of showdown between Albert and Joe. Or he's trying to prove something. I don't know. But I trust Miles. He's going to be my eyes and ears. And you and I are going to hang right here where we are in a gated community, and I have a state-of-the-art security system. I'll bring my brothers and mom in when we need to." He held her by the hips. "You have to trust me."

It wasn't that she didn't trust him, but she didn't understand why her brother would go to such lengths to keep her in the dark. "I feel manipulated. And I don't like that. When Chris was using, he lied and cheated and did whatever he had to in order to get his next fix. He put me in some pretty shitty situations. This doesn't feel all that different, except he's not doing it for drugs. But the worst part is, I don't know the motive."

Rhett took her chin with his thumb and forefinger. His gaze tore into her like a wrecking ball. "I've worked a lot of interesting cases in my career. I don't pretend to understand exactly what's going on in your brother's head right now. But I do understand love of family. And he loves you. He wants to protect you from whatever he's battling right now. He found out about you and me and what I did for a living, and he brought you to me. My job now is to protect you. To keep you safe. Miles is going to do what he can to help your brother. You've got to trust me on this. Okay?" His lips brushed across hers in a tender kiss. It wasn't romantic but it did make a statement.

"I do have faith in you and what you do for a living. But I'm scared for him. He's not a private investigator. He's not a cop. He's just a guy who worked retail and now works for a limo company, which might be run by the mob." All she wanted was for this to be over. She wanted to be able to hug Chris and Jackie and then maybe explore the idea of seeing Rhett again.

If he was open to the idea.

But that wasn't even possible for as long as her brother was on the run.

"Come on." Rhett laced his fingers through hers and tugged.

"Where are we going?"

"We're going to sit in the living room and have a glass of wine. I'll order some dinner, and we can chill and chat."

"How can you be so calm? My insides are screaming."

"Years of training," he teased. He made his way to the small bar and pulled down a bottle of red wine.

She curled up on the sofa, tucking her feet up under her butt and wrapping the small blanket around her body. Her pulse quieted. Deep down, she knew there wasn't anything she could do. Racing off to the state park and peeking her head into every campsite wouldn't do any good and wouldn't help her brother. Rhett was right about that. There was so much she didn't understand about what was going on. It made her head hurt, and her heart ache.

"Here you go." He handed her a glass and took a seat on the other end of the sofa. She stared at the large clock on the wall. It was in the shape of a gigantic sea turtle. She'd never seen anything so spectacular before. The background colors were sea blue and green and it had a coral reef thing on the bottom. The numbers were baby turtles. The only thing that looked out of place were the arms that told the time, which indicated that it was a little after six.

She would be spending another night in Rhett's house. She could push to go to a hotel, but what good would that do? And it would be depressing. Besides, Rhett wouldn't let her sit there alone. He'd be in the room with her, and all a hotel would offer was a bed and a television. At least here, she had options. Like a pool. A hot tub. A dock to sit on and drop a line if she were so inclined. She could actually get away from Rhett.

If she wanted.

Which she didn't. And that frightened her.

For the second time in her life, she found herself wanting to do something selfish. Something that only involved her needs and desires. And that came with guilt.

"What are you thinking about?" Rhett asked in a soft, gentle voice. He had this great ability to read her moods. Not many people she knew took the time to understand her emotions. Her brother had been getting better at being more aware of those around him, but he was the first to admit that it was a struggle. He'd spent his entire life being self-absorbed and all-consumed by thoughts of drugs and other destructive behaviors.

She gave her brother a pass on most things.

Something her therapist had told her she shouldn't do. At least, not anymore. She should demand respect. She had a right to have her needs met in any and all relationships. Nothing should be one-sided, and she appreciated Chris working on that.

Until six weeks ago when he started acting like an asshole.

"My mind is going in circles," she admitted. "I start off in one place and end up back to six weeks ago, trying to figure out what triggered the change in Chris."

"We know what it was," Rhett said. "He found out about Albert. Or if he already knew, Albert's secret was at risk, and he felt that if you stayed in Jacksonville, they'd use you to flush out him and Jackie."

"You really believe the best thing for you to do is simply sit here with me?"

Rhett took a big sip of his wine before setting the glass on the coffee table. He inched closer to her, putting his arm on the back of the couch behind her shoulders. "That's not what I'm doing. It might feel that way, but Miles is actively looking for Chris, and I wouldn't send someone out there if they weren't good."

"How long has Miles been working for you?"

"Part-time for fifteen years," Rhett said with pride. "Miles loves his work as a mechanic. And if you ever need someone to work on your car, he's your man. But he's like me and all my brothers."

"Adrenaline junkies?" she said with a laugh. "The things you got me to do in Key West still amaze me. I was so out of my comfort zone. I barely even went into the ocean before that, other than to wade in the water. And even when I did that, all I ever heard was the *Jaws* movie music. I could never jump in and go snorkeling. Or surfing. Much less swim with the monsters."

He laughed that rich, deep rumble of his that landed in the center of her gut and filled her insides like the warm sun coated her skin.

"I found your fears endearing. And you're not alone. Being frightened is a healthy thing."

"You don't seem to have any fear."

He cleared his throat. "I have plenty and I'm looking at one of them."

She pointed at the center of her chest. The

blood from her heart pumped faster. "Me? Why on earth would I scare you?"

He inched even closer. "Because when I'm with you, I tell myself that I'm not going to do certain things. Like this." He pressed his mouth to hers, kissing her softly. It wasn't a powerful kiss, or even a passionate one.

However, she found herself gripping his shoulders for support.

"I lose all control when I'm with you, and that's frightening." He leaned back. His chest heaved up and down as he breathed deeply. "That's not a feeling I welcome."

"You make it sound like you don't enjoy being with me." Shit. What a stupid, immature thing to say when she wasn't even sure *she* wanted to be with *him*. Loving him wasn't the issue. Of course, that was still crazy. She'd written in her diaries that she loved the idea of him but that she couldn't be sure she really loved him.

Or could she?

"*Au contraire*." He smiled, batting her nose. "Being around you is like taking a breath. It's easy. It's natural. And it's necessary. But it's so much more because my heart races, and my blood turns hot, and it becomes hard to take a deep breath." He patted his chest. "It hurts right here, and suddenly I don't know which end is up. I don't know if I'm coming or going. But what scares me the most is that I want that feeling to level off. I don't want it to be the rush I get when I jump from a plane or swim with sharks. I want it to be constant, and that's a frightening place for me to be."

She opened her mouth, but no words slipped out. Her tongue grew thick and heavy. She tried to swallow, but her muscles wouldn't cooperate. She couldn't relate to his analogy. She'd never been a thrill-seeker, except for maybe those three weeks in Key West.

Rhett had been following some guy, and the man had gone on one excursion after another. Shelby went with Rhett, not only because he asked and she wanted to spend time with him, but because doing those wild and crazy things made her heart beat a little faster.

She'd felt alive for the first time in her life.

For years, she'd only existed.

Even though she was utterly terrified for Chris and Jackie, sitting on this sofa, she realized that it wasn't only the thrill-seeking adventures that'd created those sensations.

It was Rhett.

She knew that because her blood had pumped through her system differently ever since she'd laid eyes on him again. It was a heightened awareness of self and her surroundings.

It did feel as though she was a bit out of control. However, that could be because of the situation.

Or maybe because she fought her feelings.

"Can I ask you something?" She wanted to trust her emotions and believe that she and Rhett had half a chance.

"Sure." He leaned forward and grabbed his wine glass, but he didn't scoot away. He remained close, with his knee pressed against hers.

"Have you had a serious relationship since we saw each other in Key West?"

"No," he said rather quickly. "When I came back, I knew I needed some time alone. I didn't date anyone, not even for sex, for maybe fifteen months or so."

"You love sex." Her cheeks heated, remembering how insatiable he'd been, and how she hadn't wanted to deny him. She'd never known how boring her sex life was until she met Rhett. And when she started dating again after Key West, she fell right back into what her father had called the accounting type of guy.

He'd always teased her about her taste in men. He called them safe, and her father was right. She picked guys that were reliable but not very exciting. And she got bored.

Rhett brought his hand to his forehead and chuckled. "You make it sound like I'm a horndog."

"I'm just saying that you liked starting your day with it, and often wanted to end it the same way."

"Only because I was spending time with the sexiest girl in the world." He leaned in and kissed her neck, right under her earlobe.

She shivered.

"However, I needed to focus on myself. And I had to do that alone. So, I didn't date. Anyone. And no casual sex." He paused to polish off his wine. "Eventually, I got back out there, but to be honest, I never lasted with anyone for more than a few months."

"What about before Krista? Did you have long-lasting relationships?"

He tilted his head. "My high school sweetheart lasted two years. But after that, no, not really. Why?"

"I'm curious about your life, that's all."

"All right. That's fair." He let out a long breath and leaned back. "Tell me about your love life."

She burst out laughing. "I can't say I've ever had one."

"You're thirty-five years old. You must have had relationships."

"The longest boyfriend I've ever had lasted fourteen months. We broke up because he said I cared more about my family than him, which was true. I've tried dating apps and other such nonsense, but nothing sticks." She shrugged before taking one small sip of her beverage.

"And in the last five years? Do you think of me at all when you're with these other men?" He took her glass and set it on the table. Palming her cheek, he stared into her eyes, holding her gaze intently.

She wanted to look away but couldn't break eye contact. It was too intense. Too real. Her breath caught in her throat.

"Because you're all I've ever been able to think about. For the longest time, Emmett was the only one who knew about you, so people thought I was still twisted up over Krista. But for five years, it's only been you."

She blinked.

And blinked again.

She tried to find the words to respond. To tell him that she felt the same way, but they got jumbled somewhere in her chest, and all she did was make some weird grunting sound.

He ran a thumb across her lower lip. "I've thought about you every day. But because I didn't trust myself after you left Key West, I deleted your contact information."

"Why did you do that?"

He raked his fingers through his long hair and glanced at the ceiling as if the fan swirling around had the answers. "I did some not-so-cool things when Krista broke up with me."

"Like what, exactly?"

"Like follow her and her boyfriend."

At first glance, that felt creepy, but Shelby knew him, and he didn't follow anyone without reason. "Why did you do that?"

"I have a jealous streak. I was obsessed with her. I couldn't get over her."

Shelby shook her head. "I don't believe that's the whole story. You told me she came in and out of your life. That she teased you."

"That doesn't give me the right to follow her."

"No. It doesn't. But you don't do anything without a reason." Shelby lowered her chin and raised a brow. "What did she tell you about her boyfriend?"

"It doesn't matter. What I did was wrong."

"I'm not condoning using your position as a private investigator to keep tabs on an ex, because that would piss me off. But it sounds like she was manipulative and lied to you. She made you believe something that wasn't true so she could have her cake and eat it, too."

"I agree, that's true. She *did* lie to me. And her boyfriend—now husband—is a nice guy who married a woman with some serious issues." Rhett rolled his neck. "However, I'm not proud of my behavior, and for a long time, I tried to blame it on Krista and the things she told me or the way she came in and out of my life. The bottom line is, I had an unhealthy attachment, and I needed to change things inside myself. When you drove away five years ago, I felt that same tightness in my chest. I knew there were things in your life that you were keeping from me. I could see them in your eyes. I felt them when we held each other late at night. I wanted to know what they were, but you never opened up to me, and there—"

"I could say the same thing about you."

"That's a true statement," he said. "Because I'm pretty good at my job, and I knew enough about your life that I could have found you. I thought about it more than once. But do you see how that would have looked and felt for me, considering my issues with getting over Krista?"

"I do. But you're not a stalker," she said. "While what you did was wrong, if you'd wanted to find me, using your skills to do so, and were honest about it, do you see how that would have been different?"

He shoulders moved up and down as he chuckled. "When you add the honesty factor, yes."

"What do we do now?"

"I've got an idea." He winked.

Her nipples tightened and tingled. Her skin heated. Part of her wanted to rip off her clothing, straddle him, and do it right there on the sofa. She'd never felt uncomfortable in her body, but all her senses were heightened around him, and she became a tigress. Not only did she want to please him, but she also wanted to take from him all she could. And she didn't feel guilty about it. Not one bit.

And he always seemed willing.

He tucked a piece of hair behind her ear and kissed her cheek. "I care about you. I know that's crazy; we barely know each other. But I want to change that. I want to be with you, but we can sit here and keep chatting and get to know each other more if you want."

"Wow. You've changed."

"I like to think I'm a better version of myself," he said. "But I meant what I just said. When we find your brother, and all of this is over, I don't want this to end. I want to explore things with you. I want to date you."

Her heart grew heavy in her chest. Her life was in Jacksonville. She'd lived there her entire life. It was all she knew. And yet when she thought about spending the rest of her life there, her stomach filled with bricks, and her heart turned to stone.

She broke off the embrace and stood. Making her way toward the sliding glass doors, she stared out at the moon dancing over the river. The tide was high, so the water kissed the dock. Next door, the neighbors' kids fished. She could hear them laughing.

She'd always thought that having a family of her own was a dream she'd never be able to chase. Especially in Jacksonville. There was so much pain in that town. Her mother's death. Her father's illness. And even though her brother had managed to find happiness with Jackie, there were so many reminders of his past around every corner that she found herself wanting to leave. Needing to find a safe place to land.

But she'd never been anywhere that gave her hope or a sense of freedom, except two places.

The state park in Lighthouse Cove, and Key West.

"My ego is severely bruised right now." He came up behind her but didn't touch her.

She loved that he knew exactly what to do around her and when she needed his touch and when it was best to let her lean into him, which was exactly what she did as she pressed her back against his strong, firm chest.

He wrapped his arms around her midsection.

"It's so beautiful here. And I feel safe," she said.

"I'm glad."

"I've never really had that sensation in Jacksonville. It's like all I do there is exist amongst the pain of my past. It's like I live in a world where I'm chained to my feelings of having to take care of everyone. Whereas, when I'm here, or when I was in Key West, I was able to get lost." She dropped her head to his shoulder. "It wasn't about forgetting my troubles, though I did. It was as if I became a whole person. I didn't realize that in Key West. I'm figuring it out now."

"I understand."

She turned and faced him dead-on. "Do you? Because I'm not even sure *I* get what's really going on with me. I'm scared for my brother. I don't like sitting around and waiting for something to happen. And while all that is going on, I'm having all these emotions for you that I thought were some fantasy I was holding onto because it couldn't be real. It was a thing that happened. A fleeting moment in time to never be repeated. But here we are, repeating it, and—"

He hushed her with a gentle kiss. "I don't want to repeat what we had in Key West because that had a beginning and an end." He arched a brow. "However, I don't want this to end."

Tears filled her eyes.

"Don't cry," he whispered. "I didn't mean to make you do that."

"You didn't. It's just that this is a lot to take in, and where I'm used to you coming on strong with sex, now you're laying it on with all this deep relationship stuff and…and…" If she told him what she was thinking, he'd probably run out the door, down the steps, and jump into the river. "I'm afraid to tell you how I'm feeling."

"I've thought about you every day. I've

wondered about being with you. So, if you're worried about me being weird about you thinking about that, too... Don't."

She inhaled sharply, taking in his rich scent that was a mixture of rain and earth. It was as if she'd stepped into the rainforest. "I've never felt safe anywhere until I met you, but I'm afraid it will all vanish when we find my brother."

He cupped her face. "Give me a chance to prove to you that I can be your safe harbor."

10

Shelby caved to her desires. She wasn't going to overthink it anymore. Attraction was a powerful thing, and there was no point in denying theirs any longer.

She wrapped her arms around him and let her lips do the talking. The kiss was soft and tender. It was different than anything she'd ever experienced with him. It was more sensual. More loving. While it carried the same promise of what was to come, it had so much more attached to it.

"Follow me," he whispered in a raspy voice.

"Where are we going?"

He didn't answer.

Her heart hammered in her chest as he tugged her through the kitchen.

"I thought we'd take this into the master."

"I've never seen your room."

"You didn't even peek when you had the place to yourself?" He pushed open the door and let her go first.

"That would have felt like an invasion of your personal space."

"I hope you never feel that way here again."

Her breath left her lungs as she stared at a king-size bed pushed against the far wall. A couple of throw pillows with boat-themed decor were tossed about over a navy-blue comforter. He had a chair in one corner that faced doors that opened to the pool deck, where he had a perfect view of the hot tub.

"This is amazing."

"One of the reasons I bought the place." He tossed the pillows to the side and pulled down the covers.

She stared out at the blue pool lights dancing in the water.

"The first night I slept here, I thought about you as I was dozing off." He inched closer to her, toying with the hem of her shirt.

All her fears, every single one, floated from her gut like a big white puffy cloud. They were no longer heavy storms that weighed her down. They were still there, but he helped her take them, compartmentalize them, and put them where they belonged.

She didn't have to take on everyone's problems all the time. It was okay for her to have her own life. Her own world.

And it was okay to enjoy it.

She rested her hands on his shoulders. "Flattery isn't necessary. I'm going to get naked and climb into that bed with you."

"It's not about that." He took her chin with his thumb and forefinger, brushing his lips like a feather over hers, never taking his gaze from her eyes. "I lay in that bed, wondering if you had a boyfriend or if you were married. I thought maybe it was time to reach out and see where you were in life."

For a brief moment, it felt like her heart had stopped beating. She had done for others her entire life. She always put herself second while attending to the needs of her family. For the most part, she had no regrets. She felt good about being there for her father. She'd had precious time with him in his final days, and she wouldn't trade that for anything.

"I want you to know that when I bought this house, all I could see was you in it. And now that you're here, I don't want you to leave. I know this sounds crazy, but when this thing with your brother is over, I want to give us a real chance. I don't want to date you casually. I want to be in a relationship with you. I let you walk out of my life once. I have no intention of letting that happen again."

The words she wanted to say were stuck in the past and she couldn't pull them into the present. She searched his deep, intense eyes and saw no hesitation. He was all-in, and she loved him for that confidence.

She wished she had it.

She needed time to make peace with all the hours and days she'd spent wondering and fantasizing about him so she could turn those dreams into realities.

And that started tonight.

The only way she knew how to answer him right now was with a passionate kiss. She was absolutely willing to give them a chance. But she didn't know what that looked like, and she couldn't think about it until after all this business with her brother and Jackie was cleared up.

"I take it that's a yes," he whispered in her ear as he lifted her shirt.

She took a step back, removing her top and tossing it across the room. She unhooked her bra and let it drop to the floor. "This will sound like a contradiction since I'm going to take off my pants now, but we need to take things slow."

He chuckled. "We're past that in the bedroom. But I understand, and I agree."

Biting down on her lower lip, she stood before him, completely naked. There was no other man in her past that she'd ever felt this comfortable with. This sensual with. She'd always felt good in her skin. She exercised and ate healthily. She worked to take care of herself physically. Of course, her therapist once told her that she did that better than most in part to make up for the fact that she didn't take care of herself emotionally.

Being with Rhett—deciding that having a future with him—felt like a new chapter in her psychological well-being. It was as if her heart finally had what it needed like her body did.

Her father had told her that life would come full circle one day.

This was that day.

She watched in awe as Rhett undressed, setting his cell on the table before grabbing her and kissing her hard. They tumbled onto the bed, grappling with each other, desperate to touch, taste, and please.

His lips ignited her skin as he kissed her body. He didn't miss a single inch, starting with her neck and landing on her toes. It felt as though he coated her with a layer of warm, soapy water. He washed away all her troubles.

She lost herself in their lovemaking. In his touch. She felt utterly selfish taking from him everything he had to offer. However, the few times she tried to take control, he shut her down.

He glided his fingers inside her, twisting and turning gently, his thumb rubbing her hard nub. Her hips rolled with his tender movements while his tongue rolled across her tight nipple.

Her insides tightened. The buildup started slow, curling her toes. Her calf muscles tingled. A slight tickle across her thighs eased into her core.

And then her climax slammed into her gut. "Oh, God, yes."

He brought his lips to hers, kissing her tenderly, easing himself into her as her orgasm continued to grip her body.

"Don't stop," he whispered, rolling his hips. "Keep it going." He started slowly, easing in and out, not allowing her climax to dissipate. The faster he went, the more her body demanded.

She dug her heels into the mattress and gripped

his shoulders, anticipating what was to come. Grinding against him, she tried to push him over the edge. She needed his release so she could allow her second one to explode. She was desperate for it —for him—and he didn't disappoint.

He slammed into her, grunting. He gripped her hips, holding himself there for a moment before rocking his hips in a gentle motion a few times.

"Shelby." He kissed her earlobe. "You're the girl for me."

She swallowed her breath. Her muscles burned. Her body convulsed. The space around her spun as if she were on a carnival ride.

And he rode it with her.

It took a long few moments for her to catch her breath.

He rolled to the side, pulling the covers over their bodies. "Are you okay if I leave the shades up. I like to wake up to natural light."

"I remember," she said. "Will there be anyone sneaking around the yard in the morning?"

"You can't see in the windows. They're tinted."

"That's good to know." She snuggled into his body, running her fingers over his chest. "Not to ruin the mood, but would you mind—?"

"I'm on it." He leaned away from her and lifted

his cell. "I have one text from Miles. So far, he hasn't seen your brother. He's doing a sweep with his friend, Annie. He's also obtained a list of everyone currently staying at the park and at Trapper Joe's campsite. He's also running plates and using footage of who has come and gone and when."

"Um. He can do that? Or did he get some warrant or something from your other brother?"

"My police brothers and mom don't know about this, and we need to keep it that way."

"So, this is one of those illegal things you do?"

He set his phone on some charger thing and then propped himself up on his elbow. "I try not to break the law. I might bend it; but, no. This isn't illegal. But because of how we obtained the information, it couldn't be used in a court of law, which is why I'm not telling my family right now. It's one of those it's-better-to-ask-for-forgiveness-than-permission things. Besides, the police wouldn't be allowed to get the information Miles did by greasing a few palms."

"You make it sound like you bribed someone."

"You're not that far off the mark," he said.

"Whatever you did, I appreciate it." She tucked her hands under her cheek and yawned. Exhaustion filled every part of her, but especially her mind. She could no longer hold a full thought.

He kissed her forehead. "Sleep. You need it."

"I think you're right about that." She closed her eyes and sighed. "Promise me that you'll wake me if something happens."

"I will."

She felt the bed shift. She couldn't tell if he rolled over or got out, but her eyelids were too heavy to lift.

Before tonight, she could only dream of what it would be like to have a life with Rhett.

Now that she'd had a little taste, she never wanted to let go.

11

Rhett was startled awake. His cell buzzed. It didn't ring, just vibrated on the nightstand. He blinked and stretched as he reached for his phone.

Five in the morning.

Shit.

He hadn't meant to sleep all night. He glanced to his right and smiled. Shelby was still tangled up in his sheets, purring like a kitten. As quietly as he could, he slipped from the bed, found his jeans, and hiked them up to his hips. He snagged his cell and padded out to the kitchen to make a pot of coffee.

He stopped dead in his tracks when he saw that he had a bunch of messages from Miles, and one from his mother.

Miles: *Chris and Jackie are in a camper at the state park. Her uncle, father, and mother are also in a camper at the park.*

Well, shit. That was a twist. The mother was also alive.

Also interesting that they are all together.

Miles: *I haven't approached yet. I took up residence with my friend Annie a few sites away.*

Rhett quickly swiped to the right, checking the timestamp of this message.

One in the morning.

Miles: *I'll text you if we see anything strange. For now, we're just going to watch and learn. But everything we think we know is upside down.*

Miles: *If you haven't heard, Mom made a huge bust around eleven tonight. She's got Cole Laurita in custody. You're going to want to talk to her.*

Miles: *This isn't urgent. But I've been made. I'm going to go talk with Chris now.*

Fuck.

Rhett needed caffeine before he dealt with any of this. It was a lot to take in. He also had two more texts to read. His mother's, which looked as though it'd come in around four in the morning, and the last one from Miles, which appeared to have been the one that woke him.

He'd start with Miles'.

Miles: *Chris wants you to come up here and talk. He won't tell me shit, and he doesn't want you to bring his sister. Let me know when you're on your way. He seems agitated. Something big is happening. He's scared but only wants to deal with you. Have you talked to Mom? Call her if you haven't and then get your ass up here.*

Rhett took his mug and a bagel and headed outside, sitting under his tiki hut.

Rhett: *Calling Mom now. I'll be at the park within the hour. Send me the code to get in.*

Bubbles appeared.

Miles: *8056. Come to the west side campgrounds. Site 86.*

Setting his cell on the bar, he tapped his mom's contact information. It rang once.

"Hey, Rhett. So, you came up for air?"

"Not really," he admitted. "I got a text from Miles that said you're holding Laurita and that I might want to talk to you about that."

"It's complicated. And, it's not in the news. Yet. Need to keep a lid on this for a lot of reasons, one of which affects you."

"Me?" He lifted his cold, dry bagel and took a bite. "How so?"

"We got a tip that he was picking up some

square groupers near the inlet. I went out with the Coast Guard, and, sure enough, there he was."

One of these days, he would love for his mother to use language that wasn't from the seventies and eighties, since most people had no idea that a square grouper was drugs dumped from an airplane. "No offense, Ma, but what the hell does that have to do with me? I'm not working any drug cases right now."

"Nope. But when we searched Cole's boat, we found a shitload of counterfeit money. All from the same batch as the one your girlfriend's brother had in his hotel room."

Rhett stiffened his spine. "You've got my attention."

"Cole doesn't want to go back to jail, so he asked me if we could work a deal, to which I explained that I couldn't authorize that kind of thing. But I said that if he had something good, I'd facilitate it. He told me that while he was in prison, one of his cellmates was a guy who worked for the Gorga organization, and the moment he got out, the Mortellis were at his doorstep."

"Jesus, Ma. You can't make this shit up."

"Nope. You can't," his mother said. "I had him stop because I didn't want to promise him shit that I couldn't deliver. Anyway, I've got the feds in my office right now working a bona fide deal with him."

"What do they know about my situation?" Rhett pinched the bridge of his nose. This was where things got sticky with his career and what some of his family members did.

"A little less than I do, and I'm not asking you to bring me full circle. Not yet, anyway," his mom said. "I had a brief conversation with Miles last night, and while he didn't tell me anything, he hinted just enough that I know I need to give you a little breathing room. But, Rhett, the feds are in my fucking office. You'd better not need too much oxygen, because that is a tank I can't refill."

"I'm dealing with it all this morning and should be able to loop you in shortly."

"You'd better," his mom said. "Because one of the things that Cole said in his interview with the feds was that he was the one who planted that hundred. That the Mortellis told him to."

"Why?"

"He doesn't know. Except that he was also told *not* to use the cash he was given. Well, anywhere except to plant it on Chris. Apparently, he fucked up and used it to pay some of his back bills at the marina," his mother said.

"Does he know anything about Chris? Or Jackie and her uncle?" Rhett opted not to say anything about Albert or his wife. He would have to—and probably by the end of the day, if not sooner—but for now, he'd leave things as they were.

"Only that he was to go to the hotel, ransack the room, and plant the money. Do you want me to question him about them?"

"I'd rather you didn't." Rhett leaned back and raised his mug, taking a large gulp. He picked at his bagel, dunking a piece into his coffee and letting the doughy treat soak up the heavy liquid. "At least, for as long as you can. Obviously, this is going to collide, but until I have more information—which I should have in a couple of hours—it might be better if you waited for that to happen organically."

"I'm good with that, but keep me in the loop the best you can. Got it? Don't make me chase you down."

"I won't," he said. "Listen. I have a huge favor to ask."

"You want to bring Shelby to my and Steve's house out on the island?"

He chuckled. "I'm glad you're finally calling it your house."

"Not the point," his mom said. "Why don't I swing by and pick her up? I can be there in a half-hour. Emmett and Emmerson can handle things here."

Rhett groaned. He hadn't meant for his mother to become Shelby's babysitter. He absolutely would have preferred it to be one of his brothers. Not that they wouldn't have tried to get the dirt, but they would have a hell of a lot more tact than dear old Ma. But, he figured his mom was running on fumes if she had been out all night. She likely needed to rest.

"Thanks. I appreciate it. Love you, Ma."

"Love you, too."

He ended the call and tapped Miles' contact information.

"Hey." His brother picked up before it even rang. "Thought you were just going to show up."

"I need to wake Shelby and let her know what's going on."

"You're not going to leave her there alone, are you?"

"Nope. Mom is coming to get her and will bring her back to the big beach house."

Miles laughed. Loudly.

"I'm so glad you find that amusing." Rhett tried to remember how long it'd taken for him and his brothers to stop razzing Jamison when he'd fallen in love with Bryn, or Emmett when he went bonkers for Trinity.

Rhett would never hear the end of this. And, oddly, he didn't give a shit.

"She's going to be safer there, and I'll feel better if she's with Mom while I'm having a little chat with Chris." Rhett swallowed. Shelby would be alone with his mother, who not only enjoyed playing twenty questions as she always did in cop-mode, but also tended to embarrass the hell out of her boys with all the crazy stories about them as toddlers. It made him nervous.

Especially if she got into Rhett and his inability to potty train.

He pounded his chest as if that made him a man.

"Your text mentioned that Chris was agitated. Any idea why?"

"No. He won't talk to anyone but you."

"What about Albert and Joe Staub? How are they acting?"

"Like two brothers who haven't seen each other

in years but are terrified. Whatever is going on, it's not what we first thought," Miles said. "What did Mom have to say? Is she going to insert herself in all of this? Because they will run if they see cops."

"No. She's giving me a lot of room, but that's because Cole is cutting a deal with the feds and, long story short, he's the one who was in the hotel room."

"He's always been a hired goon."

"Yup. But he's singing like a canary," Rhett said. "I wish I knew more about what was going on with that before this meeting with Chris, but at least we have Mom on our side."

"That's always a good thing."

"I'd better go. I'll see you soon." Rhett took his cell and put it in his back pocket. He stuffed the rest of his bagel into his mouth, jumped from the stool, and made his way toward the master bedroom. The center of his chest filled with the kind of thick emotion that could only be described as love.

True love.

He wanted to protect Shelby from everything in life that could hurt her, including the truth, but he knew he had to be honest with her or he'd lose her in a flash. Protecting someone didn't mean you lied to them about what was going on. However, he couldn't tell her everything because he didn't have the dots connected, and he didn't know how they affected her and her brother.

He stepped over the threshold.

Shelby turned and blinked open her eyes. She smiled. "Is it morning?" She pushed herself to a sitting position.

He set his mug on the nightstand and sat on the edge. "It is." He kissed her temple.

"Have you heard from Miles? My brother? Anyone?"

"I have." He took her hand between his palms. He didn't want to scare her, but he needed her to understand that things were getting tricky. "My mom is on her way over to pick you up."

"Where am I going, and why am I doing it with your mother?" She lowered her chin and gave him a pointed stare.

He swallowed.

"Chris wants to talk to me."

"Then I'm going with you." She swung her legs to the side of the bed."

"No. I'm sorry. You're not."

"You don't get to dictate what I do." She dropped the sheets and stood.

He groaned as she watched her pad across the

room, gloriously naked, and snag his robe off the back of the bedroom door hook. "This didn't come from me, but your brother doesn't want you there."

She spun on her heels. "I don't give a shit."

"I do." He inhaled deeply and pushed himself to his feet. He strolled across the room and put his hands on her hips. "I don't know why Chris wants this meeting. I didn't talk to him. But I know Jackie's uncle and her father are both there, as well as her mother."

"Wait, what?"

"I know," Rhett said. "There's more. My mom has the man who broke into your brother's hotel room and planted the counterfeit money in custody." He pressed his finger over her lips when she opened her mouth. "Because it's police business, I can't tell you everything. You can ask my mom about it; she might tell you more. But I don't want to leave you here alone while I go have a chat with Chris, so my mom's going to take you to her place."

"I don't need a babysitter."

"Listen. I told you I wouldn't lie to you, and I won't." He raked his fingers through his hair. "While this isn't connected like we thought, the mob is involved, and while I do have a state-of-the-art security system, I'd feel a lot better if you were with someone in my family."

"But your mother? Isn't that going to be awkward?"

He chuckled. "I'm not even going to try to downplay that one. But the more embarrassing stories she tells you about me, the more you know she likes you."

"And if all she does is give me the third degree?"

"Another sign she likes you." He took her mouth in a quick kiss. "Don't worry about my mom. She and I are working together to help your brother and Jackie. You've got to trust me on this."

She dropped her head to the center of his chest. "I do. But I feel like I have no control over anything."

"I know that's hard for you; however, this is what I do, and I'm damn good at my job." He cupped her face, tilting her head back. "I promise to protect you and your family. I'll text you as soon as I know anything."

"Thank you."

"I care so much for you," he whispered, his eyes burning. "I can't imagine life without you in it anymore."

"You really are laying it on thick now." Her dark lashes blinked over her big, blue eyes.

"I've turned into a sap in my old age."

She smiled. "I kind of like it."

"Good." He reached around and grabbed her ass. "We'd better go shower. My mother has a horrible habit of being early."

"You plan on taking one with me? When your mom is on her way?"

"I'm simply using our time wisely." He untied the robe and tugged, letting it fall to the floor. He lifted her into his arms and carried her into the bathroom.

"I have to take back my statement that you changed. You're still a horndog."

"That might never change," he said. "Not with you around." He set her on her feet, reached around into the shower, and turned on the hot water before dropping his jeans. "My God, you're gorgeous."

The water drenched their bodies. Her wet hair clung to her skin. He lifted her off the floor and pressed himself between her legs.

She arched, grinding hard against him as she nibbled on his earlobe, her hot breath driving him crazy.

There was nothing slow and tender about their lovemaking.

It was hot.

And hard.

He pressed her back against the wall, bracing himself, careful not to slip. He had no control.

Neither did she as she cried out his name, over and over again.

He felt her tighten around him, gripping him as her climax tore through her body to his, forcing his orgasm and causing him to thrust into her with such force that he nearly slipped.

It wasn't the most romantic encounter, but it was sensual, and it was filled with love.

"I'm crazy for you," he whispered.

"You're crazy, all right." She kissed his neck and sighed. "Now, let's actually get clean, so I'm not naked when I see your mother again."

12

"This is amazing." Shelby stepped into the two-story foyer of Rebecca and Steve's home.

Or maybe mansion.

Shelby guessed it to be at least eight thousand square feet. If not more.

"It's too much, and I'm trying to talk my future husband into downsizing."

"But I like it here." A handsome older man appeared. He wore khaki shorts and a golf shirt. "Hey, honey. Sorry you had a long day and night at work." He leaned in and kissed Rebecca. "You must be Rhett's girl, Shelby."

"I'm not sure that's an official title. Yet." Rebecca reached out and squeezed Shelby's arm.

"But from what little I know so far, if it is true, I would approve."

Shelby guessed that was a good sign.

"Welcome to our home," Steve said. "I'm headed out to play some golf. I'll be home for dinner."

"Unless something crazy happens in this case and my boys can't handle it, which I doubt, I should be here." Rebecca hugged her fiancé and then led Shelby through a massive great room. A wedding picture hung over the fireplace. Rebecca pointed. "That's from Jamison's wedding. The baby of the family."

"You have some seriously handsome boys."

"I'm not going to deny that." Rebecca looped her arm through Shelby's. "Let's grab a mimosa and sit out on the pool deck."

"Sounds good to me." Shelby tried not to stare at everything in the house, but it was impossible. She suspected that only the finest, most expensive things filled the home, which she found odd because Rebecca seemed like the kind of woman who didn't like flashy things.

Shelby stepped through the massive sliding glass doors from the kitchen and out onto the patio. She'd thought Rhett's house was spectacular.

But this place was breathtaking with its view of the ocean and massive pool. Not to mention the two hot tubs and the side yard with all the games and putting green.

"I know. This is all Steve. Not me," Rebecca said as she stood in front of a summer kitchen. She opened a bottle of champagne and made two mimosas. "If this weren't his dream home, I'd push harder to sell. Not to mention, my youngest boy, who happens to be Steve's biological son, loves to bring his little girl over here. All my kids like to come here with their families, and my ex-husband and his girlfriend come, too. It's become the center of our family, and I'd be a bitch if I took it away." She handed Shelby a glass. "I've worked too hard to get my boys to forgive me for my affair. I'm not going to do anything to rock the boat. And this may sound insane, but if that means living here, then that's what it means."

Before Shelby left the house, Rhett had told her to be open and honest with his mom. That Rebecca had a strong bullshit meter and hated when people weren't real. She'd rather have a difference of opinion than deal with people who had done what she'd done to her family.

Lie.

Shelby hadn't gotten the opportunity to find out what that meant since his mom had shown up, but she opted to take it at face value.

"That does sound a bit crazy," Shelby said as she took a seat in one of the lounge chairs in front of the pool, facing the ocean. "Do you mind if I ask why you don't want to live here? I mean, it's a beautiful house." Another piece of advice from Rhett was to ask questions and be genuine. Shelby had an inquisitive nature, so she went with it.

"What do you know about my history with my son, Jamison?"

"Honestly, not much."

"To make a very long story short, I had an affair with Steve while I was still married to my first husband. Rhett's father. I got pregnant. My ex and I decided to raise Jamison as ours, and Steve walked away. When it all came out, my boys couldn't forgive me. Well, Jamison couldn't. The others came around faster." Rebecca set the bottle of champagne in a cooler thing and leaned back in her chair. She raised her flute and sipped. "It was compounded by the fact that I was a bit on my high horse, believing that because my ex-husband Dalton and I made decisions that we thought were best for our family, my boys should just agree. But lying is never a good decision." She sat up taller and glanced over her shoulder. "Steve bought this house when everything in my life was upside down. Sometimes, this place reminds me of my mistakes, but then I look at that picture of my entire family with my ex included, and I wonder why I'm being so ridiculous."

"Do you want a stranger's two cents?"

"Sometimes, it's better to hear something from an unfamiliar face." Rebecca arched a brow. "Don't hold back."

"It has nothing to do with the house and everything to do with the fact that you don't think you deserve what it represents because you still don't believe you deserve Steve."

Rebecca opened her mouth but, instead of saying anything, finished her mimosa and then poured another glass.

Without the juice.

"I see why my Rhett's been all turned around about you for the last five years." Rebecca sighed.

"He told you about me?"

"No. And I had to practically beat it out of Emmett about two years ago when we found out that Krista was pregnant, and it didn't faze Rhett in the least. That's when I knew another woman had stolen his heart." Rebecca bent her knees and rolled to her side. "I liked Krista at first, but when she and Rhett broke up the first time, and I saw the devastation in my son's eyes, I was worried. It got worse when she kept coming and going and fucking with his head. I tried to intervene—something my boys hate. After that, Rhett refused to talk to me about any girl he dated." Rebecca reached out with her free hand and touched Shelby's wrist. "Though he doesn't really date much. Breaks my heart."

Shelby swallowed. This was going deep. And fast. And she wasn't ready.

But she'd been warned. She was a big girl, and the bottom line was that she had real feelings for Rhett. Ones she wanted to explore, which meant more of this and not just from his mother.

He had six brothers and a father.

"I can tell Rhett cares for you," Rebecca said. "I also know he spent a lot of time working on himself after he met you."

"He told me that." Shelby took a big gulp of courage. "When we met, neither of us was in a position to be in a relationship."

"You're right about Rhett. He was in a very bad headspace back then. But I saw how he looked at you the other day at the hotel. And I saw how you were with each other when I picked you up. It's obvious that the two of you care for each other a great deal. Rhett is a good man. He loves deeply. I can tell you do, too. I haven't always been right about the women in my boy's life, but I think I'm right when I say you're good for him, and he's the right one for you."

Tears burned in Shelby's eyes. She'd been fantasizing about that for years. She'd played out different ways of how they could meet again and fall in love.

And now, it was happening.

It was almost too good to be true.

The only thing standing in their way was this dark cloud of whatever was going on with her brother.

"I'm falling really hard for Rhett, and it's scary as hell."

"It always is when it feels like it's fast and coming at you like a freight train."

"That's a good way to describe it."

"Not to mention everything else that's going on." Rebecca set her glass down and took Shelby's hand. "Rhett and I often butt heads when our cases cross paths. We're trying to work together as best we can on this one. I know he's talking with your brother now, and I'm giving him space with that because I have no reason not to."

"I'm hoping he talks Chris into coming back to his place. I wish that—"

"I can't tell you everything. That would be irresponsible of me, so please understand that I've told you everything that I can about the case."

"I know you have, and I appreciate that," Shelby said. "I just wish my brother would have trusted me."

"Oh, sweetheart. It's not about that. It's about protecting you. And while Rhett might be more truthful than your brother, it's a different dynamic."

"I don't mean to be rude, but you don't understand. My entire life has been about taking care of Chris. I've been there for him since we were babies. And to be fair, he's never really been there for me until after he got clean and sober. Even during the first year, he didn't get how much I did or how often I worried. I know that I went too far sometimes, but still, I'm a big girl, and I deserve the truth."

Rebecca picked up the champagne bottle and refilled both their flutes. "I'm not saying you don't. But because I know some things about this, I can tell you that Chris did the right thing by keeping you in the dark and bringing you to Rhett. Where he's making a mistake is not letting my department do their jobs. I'm hoping this meeting will help show Chris that I'm going to make sure you, Jackie, and him are protected."

"Rhett can be persuasive."

"He and my eldest son, Seth, have that trait the most. They get it from their father. I always thought Rhett would have been a good lawyer. Of course, I wanted him to be a cop. He landed in the middle." Rebecca leaned forward. "I pretend I'm angry that Miles is working for him, but I'm not. I'm also insanely proud of Miles for standing up to me and opening his own business. He's one smart cookie."

"And handsome," Shelby teased.

"He's single, too. As is Emmerson. So if you know any single ladies, I trust your judgment."

Shelby laughed before taking another sip. She stared out into the blue sky as sun kissed the beach. She closed her eyes and sucked in a deep breath. "How long do you think Rhett will be?"

"As long as it takes," Rebecca said. "I need to go shower and get this work stench off me. You sit here, sip your drink, and enjoy. I'll be back shortly." Rebecca stood. "Try to relax. We're going to figure this out and get your brother back."

Shelby took Rebecca by the hand. "Thank

you."

"This might be premature, but that's what family is all about."

<hr>

Rhett pulled his Jeep up behind a dark SUV that was parked in front of a twenty-five-foot camper at the site that Miles had texted. He slid from behind the steering wheel, and a young man immediately appeared from the recreational vehicle.

"You must be Rhett," the man said.

Rhett closed the gap, stretching out his hand. "I take it you're Chris."

"Thank you for coming. Why don't we take a walk?"

"Not until I see who all is here and have a chat with my brother." Rhett glanced over his shoulder. He'd been in contact with Miles since the moment he drove through the gate. It wasn't that he didn't trust Chris, but he certainly didn't trust Albert and Joe Staub. And he didn't know Melissa, Albert's wife, from a hole in the ground. All Rhett had to go on was what he now believed were lies concocted by whoever wanted the four of them dead, and bullshit articles planted on the internet.

However, he had no idea what kind of people the Staubs really were. For all he knew, they were as crooked as kinky hair.

"I'm right here, big brother." Miles jogged across the street. He gave Rhett a manly pat on the back. "The campground is secure. My friend Annie has eyes everywhere."

"That's good to know." Rhett had a brick in the pit of his stomach. This felt off. He didn't know what or why, but he didn't like something about the situation. "Where's everyone else?"

"Inside the RV," Chris said.

"I want to see and talk with them." Rhett held up his hand when Chris tried to talk. "I know you have an agenda, and I appreciate that. But you need to understand that I'm stuck between a rock and a hard place. I have questions that need answers, and—"

"I need to protect Jackie's family. Both her uncle and her parents."

"I want to do that, too, but I need to know *why* I'm doing that. And I want to hear that not just from you but also from them." Rhett rubbed the back of his neck. "I'm here out of respect for you and because I care about your sister."

"That's fair," Chris said. "Give me a second.

Okay?"

Rhett nodded.

Chris turned on his heels and went back into the trailer.

"Have you met them?" Rhett asked his brother.

"Just Jackie. She's a sweet girl. Scared shitless, but nice," Miles said. "I have, however, seen all of them. They've had to come out of that RV to use the facilities and whatnot."

"What do you make of all this?"

"I'd be speculating since the only person Chris wants to have a conversation with is you, but when I asked him why, since I'm your brother and work for you sometimes, his only response was that Shelby trusted you. And only you." Miles stuffed his hands into his pockets.

Rhett glanced up and down the street, noting all the other trailers and vehicles. A few families sat at their picnic tables, eating lunch. A couple rode their bikes down the road. Children laughed as they raced by on their way to the playground with the parents yelling at them to slow down as they trailed behind.

A vision of him and Shelby sitting by his pool while a couple of their kids swam and played filled his head.

Suddenly, he felt like an elephant was sitting on his chest. That wasn't what he'd expected. He'd just gotten used to the idea that he was entering into a serious relationship. One that he anticipated would be his last.

Shelby was the girl for him, but he'd never thought about children.

He was forty-three years old. Granted, he wasn't an old man, and she was only thirty-five, but they hadn't even had that conversation. He suddenly became dizzy. He pinched the bridge of his nose and took in a deep breath. "What's your overall feeling about Chris?"

"I believe he's being genuine," Miles said. "I did some digging last night and this morning on the Staub family and their ties to the Gorga organization and the Mortellis."

"Did you find anything interesting?"

"Yes. Melissa is related to the Gorga family," Miles said. "It's distant, but it's there nonetheless."

Rhett didn't like that connection. "Did you tell Mom?"

"Not yet. I figured we'd bombard her all at once."

"That's probably best." Rhett glanced at his watch. He was about to go bang on the door when Chris stuck his head out and waved Rhett over.

"Good luck," Miles said.

"Stay close." Rhett adjusted his slacks, checking his weapon. He strode across the pavement and made his way up the four steps and into the trailer. Inside, Jackie and Melissa sat on one side of the small kitchen table, while Albert and Joe sat on the other side.

"Sorry it's so cramped in here." Chris stood at the end of the table. "This is my girlfriend, Jackie. Her mom, Melissa. And her dad, Albert. And that's her uncle, Joe."

"It's nice to meet you all," Rhett said. "We don't have a lot of time, and I have a lot of questions. Like, for starters—"

"We agreed to talk with you," Albert said, "because Chris trusts you. But it might be faster if we just told you our story."

"All right. I'm listening." Rhett leaned against the counter. He'd entertain this for a short period of time, but if they got longwinded or gave him a lot of bullshit, he'd interrupt and do things his way.

"Obviously, my wife and I aren't dead." Albert held his gaze. "But the world needed to think we were, especially the Gorgas."

"Why?"

"Because we wanted out. My wife wanted out, and the only way to do that was to die," Albert said. "When I married my wife, I went to work for her dad in her family's restaurant. I brought my brother with me. When her dad died suddenly—"

"He was murdered," Melissa said. "I can't prove it, but I know it's true. The Gorgas accused him of stealing and had him killed."

"Stealing what?"

"My father made counterfeit money and laundered for the Gorgas," Melissa said. "The Gorgas believed that my dad was skimming off the top. They said someone tipped them off."

"I believe that, because Melissa's father wanted out of the game, the Gorgas simply killed him because they had two new people they thought they could control," Albert said. "We were green and scared."

"Had you already known about the illegal activities?" Rhett asked.

"Of course," Joe said. "Melissa's dad told us to go along with it until he found a way to get us all out. So, we did. But that never happened, so we had to find our own way out. It took an entire year, but we thought we were fucking geniuses."

Rhett's mind was five steps ahead, and he wanted to get there as quickly as possible. "Let me guess. You decided that one of you would get in good with the Gorgas, saying that the other was stealing, and offer to kill your own brother and his wife."

"You're a smart man," Albert said. "That's exactly what we did." He waved his finger in the air. "We had a good cop friend who was willing to help us. To make sure they put a John and Jane Doe in our places, and that there was no way my brother could go down for the murder, even though we needed the Gorgas to believe he did it since he was hired to do it."

"The police report that Jackie and Chris put in the safety deposit box. Where did that come from, since it goes to the idea that Joe killed his brother and sister-in-law?"

"Pages of that started showing up on my doorstep about six weeks ago," Joe said.

"Is that why you hired Chris?" Rhett asked.

"He wanted to help. I told him no, but that kid doesn't take no for an answer too well." Joe shook his head, letting out a long breath.

"Chris, why were you sneaking around your sister's house?" Rhett rubbed the back of his neck.

"When my father was dying, I spent a fair amount of time at her place. One night, I was in her office using her computer. One of her journals was on her desk, and it was open to a page with your name on it. I read one paragraph and was floored. I've always wanted my sister to have someone in her life. She's always taken care of me, my dad, my mom, and she's never done anything for herself. I flipped through a few more pages and nearly fell over. Next thing I knew, I'd read all about her time in Key West. I couldn't believe it. So, when all this happened, I knew I needed to find you."

"I need to backtrack a bit because here's where I get confused," Rhett said. "Why did the Gorgas set Joe free?"

"That was always part of the deal," Joe said. "I went to them with what I knew, but I told them I never wanted to be part of the business. That I had taken the job not knowing what my brother's new bride or her family did. I agreed to do their dirty work if I got to take Jackie and move to Florida to start over. Unfortunately, they fucked with me from the beginning."

"How?" Rhett asked.

"The orchestrated the first loan I got to prove their reach. That made me look bad and as if I had ties to the Mortellis," Joe said. "They have always made me look over my shoulder, which was why I had to lie to my beautiful niece about her parents, and my brother and his wife have been living in Pensacola, unable to be reunited with their family."

"There had to be a trigger for the Gorgas to come after you," Rhett said. "They had to know about Albert and Melissa or—"

"That's the only thing we can think of," Chris said. "Melissa's sister passed away three months ago. She and Albert went up to New Jersey. They didn't go to the funeral, it was a month later, but someone must have seen them."

"That's when weird things like that police report started showing up at Joe's place," Melissa said. "We're sorry we dragged you into this, but that counterfeit money is a statement."

"They sent me a bundle with some of the dye that we used to make it," Joe said.

"Basically, you do what they say, Joe doesn't go to jail, and Albert and Melissa get to stay dead," Rhett said.

"Only you know that's not what would have happened." Chris folded his arms across his chest.

"Oh, trust me. I get that the Gorgas would have set up Joe to go to jail for murder, among other things, and they would have put Albert and Melissa six feet under for real." Rhett saw no reason to sugarcoat things at this point. These people had been living with one foot out the front door and eyes in the backs of their head for long enough.

That was no way to spend your life.

"This certainly sheds some light on what's been happening. I'm not sure what we do or where we go from here. But hiding out in an RV at a state park isn't safe. I need to talk to my mom, and we need to come up with a plan."

"The Mortellis and the Gorgas have a lot of people in their pockets," Albert said.

"Not my mother. Or my brothers or anyone in that office." Rhett puffed out his chest. "Before you say that everyone has a price, I'm going to tell you that's where you're wrong. Sometimes, it's not a price, because you couldn't buy any of us. Not with money."

"But you're admitting to a weak point," Joe said. "Because we all have one."

"Of course." Rhett reached out and squeezed Chris's shoulder. "That's why this one brought his sister to me. And he's with all of you. He'd do whatever they asked to protect you all—within reason because we all have a moral compass. The bad guys know that because, believe it or not, so do they. Of course, they call it a code. They know Chris here isn't going to kill anyone for them, but he might give them information to save his sister." Rhett tapped his chest. "But here's the thing. I was born and raised to defend and protect what's mine. And what's right. It's a very different mentality when you've been brought up in that environment. And while I get that there are power-hungry cops and bad people everywhere, my mom's house is clean."

"If Chris trusts you, then so do we." Albert stretched out his hand. "But we want to hear the plan before we commit."

"I'll give you the respect of that discussion. However, you need to know that once my mom is brought in, this is out of my hands," Rhett said. "Let me talk with Chris outside for a minute." He had no idea what to do with all the information that had been tossed at him in less than twenty minutes. His mother and brothers would be able to put their heads together and come up with a plan quickly. This was more their expertise than his.

He walked outside with Chris following. When he'd taken about ten steps from the RV, he turned to face Shelby's brother. "The second I call my mother, she's going to either have one of my brothers come here and escort you in, or she'll do it herself. You need protection." Rhett pointed at the RV. "Everyone inside is in danger, and you're putting this entire campground in a bad situation."

"They're terrified they'll be arrested. And there are people on the inside that will kill them in a second." Chris lifted his hand. "You and your family may be Mary Fucking Poppins, but let's face it, when the state of New Jersey finds out that you have a dead couple and that police report surfaces, they will be looking for extradition. They will make a stink, and you know the federal government will get involved."

"You're getting ahead of yourself. All that takes time, and before that, my mom would have to file reports. And she's not going to do that right away," Rhett said.

"What if the media finds out?"

Rhett had to admit that could be a problem. And it was one he couldn't control. But he could minimize the probability. "If you stroll into the station without being escorted and do it at a time where they aren't busy, which we can all be in contact about, the media won't know shit. Or we take you to a safe house and deal with it there— whatever my mom thinks is best. Because the bigger problem is that you can't keep running, and my brother Miles and I can't protect all of you and your sister from an entire mob family." Rhett raised his hand and wiggled two fingers. "Two mob families, actually."

"I believe the Mortellis have people working at the limo company. I'm sure there is an all-out manhunt for us at this point. We need to move. I feel like I've stayed here too long."

"You can't," Rhett said. "They will catch you, and they will kill you. You've got to work with me on this. And trust me."

"We both know that your mom can only keep a lid on this for so long before the feds get involved. The Gorgas have people in high places."

"I'm sure that's true. But this isn't our first rodeo. Give me a few minutes to chat with my mom."

"All right," Chris said as he glanced at the sky. "How's my sister?"

"Pretty fucking pissed off at you. Otherwise, she's good."

"Do you care about her as much as she does you?" Chris asked, shifting his gaze.

"Head over heels," Rhett admitted.

13

Rhett strolled up the street with his cell pressed against his ear. "Hey, Ma. How's it going?"

"I love her," his mother said. "We need to keep her."

He laughed. "She's not a possession. She's a person."

"You know what I mean."

Just a year ago, his mother seemed like a hard, almost mean woman. Their family had been going through a lot, and his mom had taken the brunt of it. Of course, she'd been the cause, and it took her a long time to accept how much she'd hurt everyone.

His mom hadn't been a warm and fuzzy mother. Sure, she'd read him stories and tucked him in at night. He knew without a doubt that his mom loved him and would move Heaven and Earth to protect him.

But she wouldn't always do that to spend time with him or show him how much she loved him. She missed sporting events and other important things in his life, all in the name of doing what she thought was right and best for her family.

She did teach him the value of hard work, but sometimes he'd been so starved for attention that he did some pretty stupid things.

"I hope you're not embarrassing me too much."

"I'm sure I am," his mom said. "Why are you calling me and not Emmerson or Emmett?"

"Because you're a control freak."

"That's a true statement, but I left Emmerson in charge."

"That's fair, but we're going to need the chief of police on this one," Rhett said.

"Shit," she mumbled. "I guess I need to sober up."

He pinched the bridge of his nose. His mother never got drunk. She had two to three drinks at most on her days off, but it was rare that she did any day drinking. But he suspected that interrogating Cole Laurita wasn't a typical day at work. "You started early."

"I wanted to start yesterday because it took every ounce of energy I had to keep my cool."

"I'm sure my brothers said the same thing I'm about to tell you, and—"

"Yeah. I know. Someone else could have interviewed him," his mother said. "Do you want to hear the craziest thing?"

"Sure."

"Cole apologized to me," his mother said with a shaky voice. "He told me that he's wanted to say those words to me for a long time, only the moment one of Gorga's men stepped into his cell, his life was no longer his. They have been threatening his daughter. Did you know he had a kid?"

"I did. I went to high school with the mom. Nice girl, actually. I didn't know he had anything to do with his child, though."

"He told me he's been paying his fair share of child support but staying away because he's afraid the Mortellis or the Gorgas will harm his family. He said he wanted to turn over a new leaf in prison. But the Gorgas have him by the balls. They told him that if he did a few favors for them, they'd give him his freedom, but he knows that's not true."

"Did he use that counterfeit money on purpose?"

"That's what he says. He wanted to get caught so he could blow the whistle. That way, if he ended up getting cut loose, he had plausible deniability."

"That's a dangerous game," Rhett said.

"If it's really the one he's playing."

"You don't believe him?"

"Are you fucking kidding me? The man tried to kill me. Of course, I don't trust the asshole, but every goddamned thing he told me checks out. Not one thing is off, and no matter how hard I tried to trip him up, he stuck to his story right to the letter. Cole Laurita is not that good of a liar."

"What do we know about what the Gorgas know about Albert and Melissa Staub?"

"Cole said they know they're alive. He doesn't have the details on how, but he suspects someone in the police department turned or found out about the cover-up. What can you tell me about that?"

"It was pretty clean," Rhett said. "They kept it tight. But I wish we could request the reports without throwing up a big red flag. I bet something in the documentation on the cold case isn't proper and tipped off someone who works for the Gorgas. Either way, I get the impression that the mob knew long before a few months ago that Albert and Melissa are alive."

"I agree," his mother said. "They approached Cole two years ago. The Gorgas can be patient. That's what makes them so dangerous. They're not hot-headed. They aren't street thugs who go tit for tat. They are methodical and all about the bottom line. But they will get their revenge, one way or the other."

"I'm a little nervous sitting out here at the state park. It's wide-open. Lots of access points that I can't cover. And too many people. There are kids everywhere. We need to get this group to safety."

"Cole cut a deal with the feds," his mother said. "I told them I needed forty-eight hours, and they promised me they would keep this quiet. Keep Cole in my custody in my lockup while they worked out the nitty-gritty."

"Was it a New Jersey agent?"

"Not yet," his mother said. "A special agent out of Jacksonville. His name is Pete Maz. Before I agreed to anything, I checked in with our buddy in Miami. Maz is clean, and lucky for us, he likes to bend. I'm sure I can get him to agree to a sit-down, and I know he'll go for witness protection. He knows they exist. He wants to nail Tony Gorga in the worst way. I guess he had issues with him years ago when he worked up in D.C., and it's been a thorn in his side ever since."

"Yo. Rhett." Miles waved from down the street in front of Chris's RV. "We've got company coming."

"Ma, I gotta go."

"Bring them to the station. Do it now. I'll work out the details."

"See you soon." Rhett jogged toward his brother. "What's going on?"

"One dark SUV just rolled through the gate. Annie said two men, and neither was dressed to go kayaking, biking, or hiking. She said they looked ridiculous in their Floridian clothes that screamed *tourist*. They also asked too many questions about the layout of the campsites. Something about checking it out for future reference."

"Fuck," Rhett muttered.

"Annie's got a boat. We can take that down to your place and then get to the station from there," Miles said. "The tide is going out. We've got a short window, maybe fifteen minutes before it's too shallow to get the boat downriver."

"You'd better get a move on, then." Rhett raced to the RV and yanked open the door. "The bad guys are here. Miles is going to get you all to safety."

"What are you going to do?" Chris asked.

"Follow the bad guys."

Rhett watched as Miles and the rest of the group disappeared around the corner. Only he didn't see Chris.

Shit.

Rhett turned on his heels and muttered a few more obscenities.

Chris stood by the front of the RV.

"Get the fuck out of here."

"Nope. You need backup." Chris lifted his weapon.

"Where the hell did you get that?"

"I've always had a thing for guns, but in the last two years, I've been going to the range with some of the people in my night school classes. I'm a good shot." Chris had the audacity to smile.

"You're a fucking idiot is what you are. Now, go catch up to my brother. I've got work to do." He jumped into his Jeep. He needed to park in front of where his brother had been camping about five spots down. His cell buzzed.

He pulled it from his pocket and glanced at the apologetic text from Miles about agreeing with Chris that someone had to stay behind with Rhett, and it couldn't be Miles because he needed to protect everyone else. Miles also mentioned something about Chris being a marksman, but Rhett didn't believe it.

"Motherfucking-fuck-fuck. Get in my vehicle. Now. And if you don't do what I say, I'll shoot you."

"You do that, and my sister won't be happy with you."

"If she knew I didn't force you to go with Miles, she'd kill both of us, so let's make sure we get out of this alive and make it a funny story."

"No. We're just not going to tell her."

"Don't ever ask me to lie to your sister." Rhett slammed the vehicle in reverse and drove to the other spot. He parked the Jeep. "I love her, and lying to her would be betraying her, and that's never going to happen." He jumped out from the driver's seat. His pulse popped against his wrist. It wasn't because of the situation at hand.

He loved her.

And he'd said it out loud.

Rhett glanced around. There wasn't much cover. He really didn't want to sit inside the tent, but that was really the best place at this point. He unzipped the opening. "Get in, sit down, and be quiet."

Chris didn't argue.

Rhett adjusted the window so he could see through the screen. "Did you leave anything behind in the RV they could use?"

"Nope. We gathered the important things and gave them to Miles."

"But you left all the electronics?"

"Just like you asked," Chris said. "We want this to end. Joe and Albert want to be a family again."

"You do realize that they still might have to deal with some legal issues, right? And even if we take down Tony Gorga, there will still be a target on their backs."

"And what should we do about that? Run for the rest of our lives?" Chris asked, thick emotion dripping from every word. "Their beef is with Tony only. They barely know the other people in the organization these days. No one will care."

"If they take him down, someone will have something to say. It could be good; it could be bad." Rhett kept his focus on the RV. If these men were smart, they'd have at least one come in on foot and have the vehicle roll down the street slowly from the opposite end. That could pose a problem, blocking his view for a short period of time. But all he needed to do was follow them once they left. That was the goal. Not engage them or cause conflict.

"Our plan wasn't to take them down," Chris said. "Joe honestly believed that Tony would do a trade."

"What does Joe have that Tony wants for their freedom?" Rhett rubbed the back of his neck, trying to work out the tension that filled his muscles.

"Tony has no idea that Albert took copies of the books he cooked from the business. He also has pictures of the printing press."

"That's from twenty-seven years ago. It's going to be hard for a district attorney to build a case on that."

"That's true. But he recorded conversations between him and Tony, too. And he also has video footage from the restaurant where Tony sometimes had meetings and discussed family business. Things like who he hired for what hit and other stuff that I'm sure the feds could do something with."

"Jesus. Why didn't you tell me this before? Why didn't *they* tell me?"

"Albert and Joe still think they can use it as leverage if they need to. Personally, I think they're nuts."

"Where is all this evidence?"

"In your storage caddy on your dock."

"That's what you were doing at my house. You're a little shit," Rhett mumbled. But he had to give it to Chris. He was a smart little fucker.

"I know I come off as a master manipulator. I get that. The bottom line is, this has to end. I've been trying to talk them into finding someone to trust for weeks, and the fact that they went off with Miles is a major thing. I told Miles to look there, but to make sure that Albert and Joe don't know about it."

"I have to give it to you, Chris, bringing them to Lighthouse Cove was smart for a lot of reasons. But I don't like the situation you put your sister in. All she's ever done is take care—"

"I know what Shelby's done for me. And I also know I owe her one hell of an apology. But that's between me and her."

"Perhaps. However, you stuck me right smack dab in the middle of it."

A man wearing a baseball cap, dark sunglasses, and a matching shirt and pair of shorts with turtles on them strolled from the south side of the street.

Alone.

Another man, looking similarly out of place and dressed as a tourist, approached from the north.

No vehicle in sight.

Interesting.

And not necessarily smart.

"I care about Shelby, and I'm not going anywhere," Rhett said. "How good of a shot are you really?"

"I compete with some of the best in both civilian and military marksmanship badges. I'd say I'm better than you. Not to mention, I'm studying to be a cop."

Rhett jerked his head. That was brand-new information. "How does your sister not know this?"

Chris exhaled. "As close as we are, there are things we don't tell each other. It's an odd dynamic because of our mom and my drug use and I want to change it."

"Good," Rhett said. "And for the record, My mom's hiring. She could use someone like you."

"Jackie and I were talking about how nice Lighthouse Cove is. And considering my sister is probably going to want to move here—"

"Jumping the gun, but I hope you're right." He concentrated on his breath, taking it in slowly through the nose and letting it out through his mouth. "I don't know where their SUV is, and since they know what you look like, I'm going to walk over and find out what the fuck they're doing."

"I don't think that's a good idea."

"It's not the worst." Rhett watched as one of the men walked around the back of the RV while the other tapped on the door. "Have you ever been skeet shooting?"

Chris sighed. "I've got your back."

"If I die today, your sister isn't going to forgive you."

"Nope. She'll make me suffer for the rest of my life, so let's live to see another sunrise, okay?"

"That's the plan." Rhett rolled his shoulders. Time to put an end to this bullshit so he could start the rest of his life.

With Shelby.

14

Shelby flew from Rebecca's car and raced into Rhett's house. "Chris? Jackie? Where are you?" She skidded to a stop in the middle of the family room, staring at a couple of people she didn't know.

And Jackie.

No Chris.

She turned to Miles. "Where's my brother?"

He shrugged and turned.

Jackie stood. "He didn't tell me he was going to stay behind." She inched closer to Shelby, standing about a foot away. "I would have stopped him if I'd known what he was planning."

"You couldn't have," a man, who Shelby knew

as Jackie's uncle, said. "He's strong-willed, and Miles agreed with his plan."

"You what?" She turned back to Rhett's brother and glared. "Why? My brother's not a cop or a private investigator." She waggled her finger at Miles. "And if you start in on his gun skills, I'll find a weapon and shove it where the sun doesn't shine."

"Wow. I like this side of you," Rebecca said from somewhere on the other side of the room. "However, there's nothing we can do. What's done is done."

Shelby's blood turned to fire in her veins. Her brother had always had an obsession with guns, and it drove her crazy. When he was using, she'd stressed that he'd do something stupid.

Sober, she just worried.

"It was bad enough that I knew my boyfriend was out there following a bunch of thugs around. But now it's my brother *and* Rhett?" She rubbed her temples.

"Chris has gotten us this far," Jackie said.

"My niece is right." Jackie's uncle leaned forward from his perch on the reclining chair. "He's done things for us that no one else has."

The other man, who looked a lot like Joe, pushed

from the sofa. "He knew to bring us to Lighthouse Cove. He's kept all of us safe for weeks. He's a very smart man, and he'll do well in this line of work."

"Excuse me?" Shelby blinked.

Jackie took her hand. "He didn't want to tell you until he was done, but he's been taking college classes at night."

Shelby gasped. Her brother was full of secrets lately.

"He's only got one semester left in criminal justice. He wants to be a police officer," Jackie said with a beaming smile and tears running down her cheeks. "He wants to make you proud."

"I'm hiring," Rebecca said. "If you are willing to relocate. And Chris will have to learn not to go rogue like this again."

Shelby's breath hitched. This was not where her brain needed to be right now. She turned and stared at Rebecca. "What's the plan?" She decided to direct her attention to the problem at hand. She'd deal with all the other stuff when she came face-to-face with her brother.

Rebecca planted her hands on her hips. "I'm going to bring Albert, Joe, and Melissa back to the station. It's the safest place for them. Jackie can stay here with you and Miles, or she can come with us.

It's up to her, as long as she understands that I will need a full statement from her later."

"I want to stay with Shelby for now, if that's okay," Jackie said.

Rebecca nodded.

"What about Chris and Rhett?" Shelby asked.

"Emmerson and Emmett are at the state park. It's watch and wait right now," Rebecca said. "We take our cues from them." She waved her hand at the front door. "We need to get going while we have the bad guys contained at the park."

Shelby wrapped her arms around her middle.

Jackie hugged her family.

Her parents.

That thought filled Shelby's heart with a wave of sadness and regret. She missed her father so much it hurt her soul. But seeing Jackie reunited with her flesh and blood filled Shelby with gratitude. Shelby had so many happy memories that she wouldn't trade for anything.

Not even those five years between Key West and now.

Everything happened for a reason.

Her father used to tell her that all the time, and now she fully believed the statement.

Her life had come full circle.

Miles closed the door.

"Did you tell your mother about all the evidence?" Jackie asked.

Miles nodded.

"What are you talking about?" Shelby shifted her gaze between Jackie and Miles, her stare narrowed.

"Information that will help my mother nail Tony Gorga to the wall and protect Albert, Melissa, and Joe," Miles said. "I want you to know that I left your brother behind without my brother's blessing, but I know it was the right thing to do. Rhett was outnumbered and outgunned. I didn't know how fast my mom could get Emmerson and Emmett in place, and there is only so much they can do."

"I don't like being in the dark, and I sure as shit don't like being lied to." Shelby made her way to the sliding glass doors and stared out over the pool toward the river. The sun beat down on the ripples as an easterly breeze came across the water. A couple of otters swam by.

"I don't believe Rhett has lied to you," Miles said. "He didn't know about all this stuff."

"I'm sorry." Jackie curled her fingers around Shelby's biceps. "I know I put everyone in a bad situation. This is all my fault."

"No." Shelby shook her head. "I'm not blaming you for any of this. You were a child when your parents and uncle made the decision to do what they did. We're all pawns in this." She pulled Jackie in for a hug. This was the woman that Chris had chosen to be with. This was the love of his life, and the fact that Chris was willing to risk it all said a lot. "I'm glad you're safe. I've been worried sick about the two of you."

"I wish we didn't have to do that to you." Jackie leaned back and lowered her chin. "My uncle one hundred percent believed that the Gorga family would come after you to get to us, and since Chris started working with my uncle and was dating me, they knew they could control all of us."

"Did they threaten me?" Shelby asked.

"Yes," Jackie said. "In some of the things they started sending us, along with that fake police report were hints of other things they knew. One was a piece of paper with your address on it."

"Miles, what are my brother and Rhett going to do? How worried do I need to be?"

"I wouldn't have left them if I didn't believe in both of them." Miles rubbed the back of his neck.

It was something that Rhett did when he was

either nervous or didn't want to answer truthfully but would anyway.

"Rhett's plan was to follow the bad guys and keep us posted on where they went. But Chris just texted me that they showed up at the campground on foot, no car in sight. As we speak, Rhett's crossing the street to have a little chat with them."

"That can't be good," Shelby muttered.

Miles stared at his cell, tapping on the screen. "I'm letting Emmerson know what's going on. The good news is, our brother Nathan just returned from vacation but is still off duty. He's going to join Rhett and Chris while Emmett and Emmerson are in uniform, doing their thing."

"Why can't they just arrest them?" Shelby asked.

"They don't have cause. And we don't even have names for who these men are. We don't know if they're wanted for anything or not. If we harass them, we're fucked," Miles said. "For now, the three of us sit tight in the house unless someone tells us otherwise."

"I'm going to go fucking crazy." Shelby folded her arms and focused on the coconut trees. The fruit wasn't ripe yet, but it would be awesome to snag a few when they were and stick a straw in one to drink the milk.

"This is going to be over today," Miles said. "At least, our part of it is. My mom's going to take care of the legal issues plaguing Jackie's family, and these thugs are going to get what's coming."

In part, that's what concerned Shelby.

Rhett's phone buzzed half a dozen times in his back pocket, but he wasn't about to pull it out. Not when two of the bad guys were staring him down with frowns on their faces.

"Can I help you?" Rhett said as he approached Chris's RV.

"I think we should be asking you that," one of the men said as he folded his arms across his chest. He stood tall in front of the door.

Rhett might as well draw the battle lines. "This is my future brother-in-law's campsite. So, I'll ask again. Can I help you with something?"

"Why, yes, you can," the other man said, inching closer. "My name's Angelo. That guy over there's my cousin, Frankie. We're looking for Chris and Jackie, and Jackie's uncle Joe. Now. We know they're here. So, let's not play games. Just tell us where they are."

"They aren't here," Rhett said. "Why are you looking for them?"

"That's our business," Frankie said. "Not yours."

Rhett shrugged. "Guess I can't help you."

Angelo lifted his shirt, showing off his big gun. "That's not smart," he said in his Jersey accent.

"You do know you're in Florida, right?"

"What does that have to do with anything?" Angelo narrowed his stare.

"Everyone in this state is packing. And it's perfectly legal to carry concealed weapons if you have a permit. Now, I'm betting you don't have one for that since you're not from Florida. I'm not a cop, but I know a few."

"We're not afraid of some local police officers."

Rhett wanted to laugh. "All right. But you should be very frightened of me."

Angelo closed the gap, getting right in Rhett's face. "You're nothing to us, and we'll break your legs without thinking twice."

"That wouldn't be a smart play," Rhett said calmly. "What is it that you want with Chris, Jackie, and Joe?" He held his ground, his nose scant inches from Angelo's. It took all the positive energy he could muster not to punch him in the face. "Just tell me. Maybe I'll be inclined to share what I know."

Angelo tipped his head. "If you were smart, you'd tell us where he is right now. Otherwise, we're going to have to get it out of you the hard way."

"And if I'm not so bright?"

"We'll beat it out of you," Frankie said.

"I'm not a fan of that option," Rhett said, holding up his hands. "I'm going to reach into my back pocket and pull out my cell to text Chris. I don't have his exact location, but I can get it."

Frankie put his hand on his weapon. "You'd better not fuck with us or else."

Rhett wanted to ask the *or else what?* question but opted to refrain from sarcasm. That never ended well, and he didn't really feel like taking a punch to the gut. The old Rhett would have done exactly that because feeling a little physical pain let him know he was alive.

Now, just picturing Shelby in his mind gave him the same sensation.

"Okay. So, I'm texting Chris," Rhett said, not too loudly but with a fair amount of inflection. Because he didn't have Chris's contact information, he couldn't actually do it, but he would send a group message to all the important people.

His mom and his brothers, including Miles. And then he remembered the number that Chris had set up for his sister to use. That might work to contact him.

He quickly drafted that text, letting them know he had engaged the enemy.

He stole a glance at the few texts from Emmerson about Nathan being in the park, off duty, and that he had eyes on the vehicle at the north end of the circle where the campground started.

And that it was empty, with the keys inside.

Nathan was currently moving it.

That was good.

Miles had also texted a long update about the situation at the station. Rhett didn't have time to read it all. Keywords had to do with five arrests in the Mortelli organization and that Tony Gorga might not have had anything to do with the fake police report, but that it may have been a disgruntled member of his organization who'd been in prison until a year ago.

That was an interesting piece of information that Rhett could use. That meant this entire thing took on a different twist. If Tony Gorga hadn't ordered this, and it was coming from somewhere else, that was both good and bad. Good because Tony Gorga might be a criminal, but he had a code. If Joe had been given walking papers, he'd stick with it.

Of course, there was the Albert thing to deal with, too. That still might be enough to piss off Tony Gorga.

Maybe.

Rhett glanced over his shoulder, staring at the other site. He gave a slight head jerk, hoping that Chris saw and understood that it meant for him to get the fuck out of the tent.

With his weapon.

"I'm telling him that this is where the fun begins because we're not only going to fuck with you, but we're also going to take you down," Rhett said.

"Excuse me?" Frankie drew his gun, lunging in Rhett's direction, shoving it into his side.

Rhett grunted.

God, he hated the way metal felt, even when there was fabric between it and his skin.

"Who do you work for?" Rhett asked as Frankie patted him down, removing his weapons.

All of them.

Fucker.

"Someone you don't want to mess with."

"I know it's not Tony Gorga, and when he finds out you're down here—"

"Shut the fuck up." Frankie backhanded him with the butt of his weapon.

Out of the corner of his eye, Rhett saw his brother Nathan slip into the tent.

Okay. Chris had a pass for not coming to his rescue right now.

"Start walking." Frankie shoved him.

Rhett raised his hands. "Why don't you just answer my questions? What difference does it make at this point? You're just going to shoot me and dump my body on the side of the road for the alligators."

"We don't want you. We want Joe Staub. Tell us where he is, and you can go."

"I've been around the block too many times. I know that's bullshit." Rhett's cell buzzed in his hand. He glanced at the screen at what looked like a five-page note.

Nathan: *With Chris. Watching. Big news. Gorga has always known about Albert and Melissa. He gave them their freedom a long time ago. They were on his no-bother list. Hector Mortelli took issue with that twenty-seven years ago* *when he wasn't allowed to force Joe Staub into helping him set up his business in FL. Gorga has been able to keep him under his thumb until Cole spent time in a federal prison. Keep them talking. Mom's crossing every—*

"Reading a novel?" Angelo reached for Rhett's phone.

Rhett jerked his hand. "Just some interesting facts about the two of you," he said. "So, you work for Mortelli and not Gorga. That's interesting." Rhett didn't quite understand what was taking so long for his people to move in, but he was just glad that he hadn't taken a bullet for his troubles. Because these guys were about to get trigger-happy.

"Where the fuck are you getting your facts, and what the hell is it to you?" Angelo pushed his weapon harder into Rhett's ribs.

Nathan stepped from the tent. Chris was right behind him but crouched down, and he quickly ducked behind the Jeep while Nathan strolled down the street.

The sound of a twig cracking caught his attention. He did his best not to jerk his focus.

Emmerson hid in the trees in his uniform, weapon drawn.

Emmett was somewhere close.

It was about to go down.

Whatever they needed to make sure the legal aspects were taken care of, and he didn't get caught in the crossfire…he was good with it.

"I'd appreciate it if you took that fucking thing out of my side." Rhett took a step back.

Nathan double-timed it with his weapon pressed against his leg.

A police car came around the south side of the bend. Another around the north side. People scattered.

Angelo grabbed Rhett and pressed his gun into his temple.

Rhett lifted his hands. "You're making a big fucking mistake," he said through gritted teeth.

Frankie aimed his weapon toward Nathan. "Don't come any closer, or this asshole dies."

"There's no way out," Nathan said. "This entire campground is surrounded."

Rhett swallowed. He wouldn't feel like this was over until he no longer felt something cold and hard against his body.

Emmerson made himself known. "Drop the weapon," he said.

Emmett rolled his patrol car to a stop. He eased from behind the wheel. "Release Rhett and place your guns on the ground. We're not going to ask you again."

"Shit," Angelo muttered. He gave Rhett a good shove.

Thank God. Before anything went crazy, Rhett snagged Angelo's weapon. He had half a mind to smack the fucker across the face. But that wouldn't get Rhett anywhere but maybe a good lecture from his brothers.

And, ultimately, his mother.

"I'll take that." Nathan took both Frankie's and Angelo's guns.

Emmerson took out his handcuffs, as did Emmett.

Chris came out from behind the Jeep and strolled across the street.

"There's that little fucking asshole." Angelo lurched forward.

"Not a good idea." Nathan got in his way, holding him back. "Read these two their rights and get them out of here."

"On it," Emmett said. "See you guys later." He slapped the metal bracelets on Frankie.

Emmerson took care of the other goon.

Rhett rolled his neck, giving it a good rub.

"You all right, little brother?" Nathan slapped his shoulder.

"Fucking wonderful," Rhett said. "How was your vacation?"

"It was great. But, damn, does a lot of stuff happen while I'm gone. Like Mom told me you're all in love or some shit."

"Yeah. With my sister." Chris joined them in front of the RV. "I didn't intervene because your brothers told me not to."

"I get that." Rhett inhaled sharply, letting the breath out slowly. "I have a headache. What the hell is going on? Is Tony Gorga not involved?"

"He is, and he isn't. But I came to this party late. I literally landed at two in the morning and Ma was knocking on my door first thing. Why don't we head to the station and get all the answers you want? I know Mom wants to talk with this guy."

"I want to see my sister," Chris said. "Before I spend hours having conversations with police, the feds, whoever."

"I can make that happen." Rhett lowered his chin and raised a brow, staring at Nathan.

"Fine. I'll go to the station. You take Chris back to your place, but don't make her wait too long."

"I won't. I promise." Rhett grabbed Chris by

the back of the neck and led him toward the Jeep. "If you ever make your sister worry about you like that again, I'm going to be the one letting *you* stand with a gun pressed to your side."

"That's fair," Chris said. "But if you hurt my sister, I won't hesitate to be the one—"

"Yeah. This chest pounding could go on all day." Rhett laughed as he climbed behind the steering wheel.

"Is your mom really hiring?"

"Finish your degree, go through the training, and don't piss her off, and she'll hire you." Rhett turned and smiled. "If I tell her to."

"I'm going to like living in Lighthouse Cove."

Rhett would like hanging out with Chris.

Shelby sat on the edge of the pool with her feet dangling in the warm water. The sun beat down on her face.

Her brother sat next to her, sipping from a bottle of water. "I hate it when you're this quiet. It always means you're super angry," he said.

"I'm only upset about one thing." During the last hour, Miles had kept her informed of every detail. She appreciated his honesty, and she knew it came from Rhett.

It was his desire to make sure she didn't worry any more than she already had in a situation that she didn't understand.

She loved Rhett with all her heart.

Same with her brother.

Chris was her only family—her only flesh and blood—left.

Rhett was who she chose to be with. He'd become her safe harbor. Him and this quaint little town of Lighthouse Cove.

Her brother leaned into her with his shoulder. "Come on, sis. Talk to me. I know you were scared for me, and I know I put you in a shitty situation. But I really didn't have a choice. I couldn't just tell you what was going on when I didn't even know who was after us. And it's a good thing since it turned out it wasn't exactly who we thought."

She sucked in a deep breath, filling her chest with as much oxygen as possible. She held it for ten seconds before letting it out slowly. "I could have lost you. And Rhett, too."

"Shelby, I had to run. And after finding out about Rhett, I knew he would keep you safe. I won't apologize for that," Chris said as he kicked his feet. Water gently sloshed against the side of the pool.

"This might sound petty, but I resent how you found out about him."

"Are you talking about your diaries? I'm sorry, but had I not stumbled onto those, I hate to think where we might be right now."

She agreed. But that didn't change her emotions. "You invaded my personal space by reading them." She held up her finger, hushing her brother. "You violated both my and Rhett's privacy."

"I did," Chris said. "But that's not something I'll apologize for. Because without Rhett, we might not be sitting here right now having this conversation, and Jackie might not have the chance to have her family back." Chris shifted, setting his bottle down. "And you know what else? It hurt me that I never knew about him. And other things. I hate that you felt—*feel*—like you can't share your life with me. I'm not the same man I was five years ago, and I want you to lean on me as much as I lean on you. But you never open yourself up. Rhett is proof of that."

"I didn't tell you about Rhett because I didn't think I'd ever see him again." She swiped at her cheeks. "I kind of wanted to keep him in a safe bubble all to myself."

"You fell in love with him when you met him, and it's obvious he fell for you, too," Chris said. "The fact that you spent five—"

"That was for the best. For both Rhett and me. And I didn't tell you because we were dealing with so many other things."

"It's not really Rhett. It's everything. You can't keep shutting me out," Chris said with heavy emotion. "You say that I did that to you, and you're right. I did. But you have been keeping me at arm's length since I got clean. No matter what I do, it's like you're waiting for me to fail."

Tears burned her dry eyes. She shifted her gaze, palming her brother's cheek. In a few short days, she'd learned so much about herself, her brother, and about love. "All I've ever known is the pain of people letting me down. Mommy wasn't ever there for us. You checked out when you were a teenager, and while Daddy was sick, I felt like I was the only one who could take care of him."

"That's just it. You never let anyone help. Not even when I had my head on straight. You always treat me like I'm a child. I'm a grown man, and I've come a long way."

"I know. And I'm sorry for that. It wasn't my intention to make you feel that way. I was protecting myself from being hurt, and I hurt you in the process."

He took her hand and kissed it. "I love you, Shelby. You're my big sister. I want you to get to know Jackie because I'm going to marry her. I want us to be one big happy family."

"I want that, too." She let out a long breath. "I hope her uncle and parents aren't going to be in too much trouble."

"According to Miles, they'll be fine." Chris chucked his fist across her chin in a little love tap. "Rhett seems like a real stand-up guy. I hope the two of you are going to give this rekindled spark a real shot."

"We've talked about dating, and I think we both want that, but we have some things to discuss." She turned.

"Why are you still angry with me?"

"It's not anger. It's hurt. But I want you to know I'm proud of you."

"Ah. Me going back to school. I wanted to surprise you," Chris said. "But I'll be honest with you, I was afraid you'd give me a lecture and not necessarily believe I'd follow through with it."

She laughed. "I do that, don't I?"

He nodded.

"I'll work on that."

"So, are you going to move to Lighthouse Cove?" he asked.

Her heart hammered in her chest. "I think it's too soon to make that call. However, I believe it's safe to say I'm going to be making a lot of trips down here in the near future."

Chris jerked his head. "Speak of the devil. Here he comes."

She glanced over her shoulder.

"I hate to break up this party, but Miles needs to get Chris to the station. My mom needs to take his statement."

Chris jumped to his feet. "I want to thank you for everything." He stretched out his arm.

"You act like I'm not going to see you in a few hours." Rhett shook his hand. "Miles will bring you and your family back here after my mom and the feds are done. Hopefully, it won't be too late. I'll grill up some steaks. We'll have some drinks at the tiki bar. I'll make sure all the guest rooms have clean sheets. And—"

"I don't want to put anyone out. We can stay—"

Rhett cut Chris off. "It's done. Now, get out of here. My mom doesn't like to be kept waiting."

Chris smiled. He turned on his heels and headed inside, where Miles waited.

Rhett sat down next to Shelby and kissed her cheek. "Did you have a nice chat with your brother?"

"I did. Thank you for giving us a little time to talk."

"Good. I'm glad."

"What's going to happen now? I'm not sure I understand everything. Like who was after them and why."

"You didn't ask your brother?"

She shook her head. "We talked about other things."

"I see." Rhett leaned back, resting on his hands. "There are things we're never going to know, but when Joe and Albert devised their escape, they set up an insurance plan, but that was interrupted when they believed that Tony Gorga knew about what they had done. Only it was Hector Mortelli who made them believe it wouldn't ever be safe for them to be reunited. Of course, Hector had another reason to be worried."

"What's that?"

"Albert and Joe have him on tape admitting to betraying Tony Gorga. That was why he believed he was working with Gorga when Cole Laurita was in prison, when it was actually more of Mortelli's people. This whole thing was about Hector getting his revenge for feeling as though he'd been snubbed by the Gorgas. With the help of the feds, my mom's been able to arrest sixteen people in the Mortelli organization. All thanks to Joe and Albert. And, of course, your brother and Jackie. Sadly, Tony Gorga and those of his organization in New Jersey won't do any time since he's cooperating, and the feds don't have anything on him that would put him away long term. But for now, the Mortellis and the hold they have in south Florida has come to an end."

"Are my brother and Jackie safe?"

"I haven't had more than a few texts with my mom, but yes. She believes that this has been contained."

"Even with this Gorga guy in New Jersey?"

"According to her contacts, he's been trying to legitimize his businesses for the last ten years. No one is after Chris or Jackie or anyone in her family. They can start over wherever they want."

"You have no idea what a relief that is." She

sighed. "I can't believe my baby brother wants to be a cop." She shook her head. "He's always been fascinated with police shows and shit like that. But I never, in a million years, thought he'd pursue something like that."

"Based on what I've seen, he'll make a fine one, and this town could use a few more of them." Rhett sat up taller, looping his arm around her waist. "Which brings me to a very important discussion we need to have."

"Oh, yeah? What's that?" The way he smiled at her made her pulse soar.

"I thought I'd take some time off work. I understand you might not have any more days off, so I can come up to Jacksonville and hang out for a while if you'll let me. I just think we need to spend some time together."

"I'd like that very much." She leaned into him. "I look forward to us spending a lot of time together."

"I know long distance can be hard, but I'm willing to put the time in. I want to see where this takes us." He kissed her cheek. "Is it too soon to say I've fallen in love with you?"

"That happened five years ago to both of us." She smiled. "But now we need to slow down and enjoy what that means and really get to know each other. I mean, I don't even know your favorite color."

"Blue. Like your eyes."

She dropped her head to his shoulder.

"Next question," he said.

"Is the house empty?"

"I believe so. Why?"

"Well, if my brother and Jackie and her family are staying here tonight, and tomorrow is Friday, that means it might go on for the weekend. Knowing me and Chris, you and I might not have a lot of alone time for the next few days."

He tilted her chin, brushing his lips over hers. "You know, I said the words. But you didn't."

"I'm falling in love with you all over again," she whispered. "Call me crazy, but this is where I belong."

15

TWO MONTHS LATER...

*R*hett pushed the dresser up against the wall in the master bedroom. Shelby had moved in last week, but they were still figuring out where to put half her furniture.

He'd finally given up the fight and put his so-called *masculine bachelor set* in one of the guest rooms and gave another set to the Goodwill.

She also managed to talk him into giving up the living room set, which he did have to admit was dated, while they moved in her newer set.

"I told you this was nicer." She lay on the bed with her ankles crossed as she sipped a bottled water, wearing a robe.

When did that happen? The last time he'd

looked at her, she'd been in a pair of shorts and a T-shirt.

"Do you have anything on under there?" He circled his finger.

"My swimsuit," she said. "The hot tub is heating up."

"I see," he said. "So, while I've been busting my ass moving all this stuff around, you've been lounging and waiting to soak."

"You're welcome to join me."

He chuckled. "I plan on it." He patted his front right pocket. Thankfully, it was still there. He'd been worried he would lose it all day. Of course, she'd been barking orders at him all day, and he *had* promised her he'd use the weekend wisely to make sure that all her stuff was finally in place.

This would be their first official week living together.

But he wanted more.

He wanted a life. A family.

And it all started with a simple question. He was confident that they both wanted the same things, which was why she'd moved in. But it was still nerve-wracking.

He sat on the edge of the bed and pushed aside the robe, resting his hand on her sexy thigh. "I'm excited for your brother to enter the police academy."

"I can't believe he bought a house in this neighborhood. Are you sure you're okay with it?"

"Of course. It will be great to have him and Jackie as neighbors. But I thought maybe we should beat them down the aisle." He stuffed his hand into his pocket and pulled out the diamond ring his mother had helped him pick out. He held it up under Shelby's nose.

She gasped, covering her mouth with both hands. "Are you kidding me? Is that an engagement ring?"

"It sure is." He took her hand and slipped it onto her ring finger. It sparkled as brightly as her eyes. "I love you. I want to spend the rest of my life with you. Let's get married."

"I love you right back." She cupped his cheeks and kissed his mouth. Hard. "But we need to talk about something."

"Um. Is there a chance you might say no?" He arched a brow.

"Oh. I'm saying yes. I want to marry you. And we should do it as soon as possible. I don't want a big wedding. I'm happy to get on the boat and drive to the Bahamas next weekend to do it."

He groaned. "I don't need a big one, either, but I do need my family. And since not all of the cops in my family can have the same day off, would you be willing to have a beach wedding here?"

"That's fine. Are you good with doing it as soon as possible, though?"

"Name the day. I'll be there," he said.

"Good, because I don't want to be fat when I get married."

"Do you plan on doing a lot of eating between now and the wedding?"

She took his hand and placed it on her abdomen. "I am eating for two."

"Huh?" He blinked. "What does…two?" He glanced between her face and her stomach. "A baby? You're having a baby?"

"I'm having it, but *you're* going to be a daddy."

"How did that happen?" What a dumb question. "Scrap that. I know how it happened. I'm just surprised. Shocked. We only talked about having a family a couple of times. Like in the future."

"The real question is…are you happy?"

He wiped away a tear that rolled down her cheek. "Of course, I am. I told you that I didn't want to wait too long. I'm not getting any younger." He untied the robe and rested his head against her stomach. "There's really a little person growing in there?"

She ran her fingers through his hair.

"There really is."

Rhett wrapped his arms around his future wife and unborn child. He closed his eyes and took a deep breath. His mother always told him that everyone needed a safe harbor to sail into.

This was his.

ABOUT THE AUTHOR

Jen Talty is the *USA Today* Bestselling Author of Contemporary Romance, Romantic Suspense, and Paranormal Romance. In the fall of 2020, her short story was selected and featured in a 1001 Dark Nights Anthology.

Regardless of the genre, her goal is to take you on a ride that will leave you floating under the sun with warmth in your heart. She writes stories about broken heroes and heroines who aren't necessarily looking for romance, but in the end, they find the kind of love books are written about :).

She first started writing while carting her kids to one hockey rink after the other, averaging 170 games per year between 3 kids in 2 countries and 5 states. Her first book, IN TWO WEEKS was originally published in 2007. In 2010 she helped form a publishing company (Cool Gus Publishing) with *NY*

Times Bestselling Author Bob Mayer where she ran the technical side of the business through 2016.

Jen is currently enjoying the next phase of her life…the empty nester! She and her husband reside in Jupiter, Florida.

Grab a glass of vino, kick back, relax, and let the romance roll in…

Sign up for my Newsletter (https://dl.bookfunnel.com/82gm8b9k4y) where I often give away free books before publication.

Join my private Facebook group (https://www.facebook.com/groups/191706547909047/) where I post exclusive excerpts and discuss all things murder and love!

Never miss a new release. Follow me on Amazon:amazon.com/author/jentalty

And on Bookbub: bookbub.com/authors/jentalty

His Deadly Past

The Corkscrew Killer

Brand New Novella for the First Responders series

A spin-off from the NY State Troopers series

PLAYING WITH FIRE

PRIVATE CONVERSATION

THE RIGHT GROOM

AFTER THE FIRE

CAUGHT IN THE FLAMES

CHASING THE FIRE

Legacy Series

Dark Legacy

Legacy of Lies

Secret Legacy

Emerald City

INVESTIGATE AWAY

Colorado Brotherhood Protectors

Fighting For Esme

Defending Raven

COLOR ME SMART

COLOR ME FREE

COLOR ME LUCKY

COLOR ME ICE

COLOR ME HOME

Search and Rescue

PROTECTING AINSLEY

PROTECTING CLOVER

PROTECTING OLYMPIA

PROTECTING FREEDOM

PROTECTING PRINCESS

PROTECTING MARLOWE

DELTA FORCE-NEXT GENERATION

SHIELDING JOLENE

SHIELDING AALYIAH

SHIELDING LAINE

SHIELDING TALULLAH

SHIELDING MARIBEL

The Men of Thief Lake

REKINDLED

DESTINY'S DREAM

Federal Investigators

JANE DOE'S RETURN

THE BUTTERFLY MURDERS

THE AEGIS NETWORK

The Sarich Brother

THE LIGHTHOUSE

HER LAST HOPE

THE LAST FLIGHT

THE RETURN HOME

THE MATRIARCH

More Aegis Network

MAX & MILIAN

A CHRISTMAS MIRACLE

SPINNING WHEELS

HOLIDAY'S VACATION

Special Forces Operation Alpha

BURNING DESIRE

BURNING KISS

BURNING SKIES

BURNING LIES

BURNING HEART

BURNING BED

REMEMBER ME ALWAYS

The Brotherhood Protectors

Out of the Wild

ROUGH JUSTICE

ROUGH AROUND THE EDGES

ROUGH RIDE

ROUGH EDGE

ROUGH BEAUTY

The Brotherhood Protectors

The Saving Series

SAVING LOVE

SAVING MAGNOLIA

SAVING LEATHER

Hot Hunks

Cove's Blind Date Blows Up

My Everyday Hero – Ledger

Tempting Tavor

Malachi's Mystic Assignment

Needing Neor

Holiday Romances

A CHRISTMAS GETAWAY

ALASKAN CHRISTMAS

WHISPERS

CHRISTMAS IN THE SAND

Heroes & Heroines on the Field

TAKING A RISK

TEE TIME

A New Dawn

THE BLIND DATE

SPRING FLING

SUMMERS GONE

WINTER WEDDING

THE AWAKENING

The Collective Order

THE LOST SISTER

THE LOST SOLDIER

THE LOST SOUL

THE LOST CONNECTION

THE NEW ORDER